2 Elizabeths

Volume I: Love & Romance

2 Elizabeths, Volume I, Love & Romance by 2 Elizabeths LLC

Published by 2 Elizabeths LLC

ISBN: 978-1-7321091-0-0

Table of Contents

Labor of Love: A Letter from the Editor......................v

Fiction......................vii

    Making Lemonade - *Catherine Brown* 1

    The Shoebox - *R.B. Frank* 9

    The Message - *James Magner, MD*......................13

    Sea Glass - *Brandi Willis Schreiber* 23

    The Triple Lutz - *K.D. Van Brunt*......................43

    Love at First Sight - *Elizabeth G. Walzel*......................65

    Auld Lang Syne - *Gerald Winter*......................83

    Romance Novel - *Nancy Young* 101

Flash Fiction 121

    In a Castle in France - *Julia Ballerini* 123

    Night Owl - *Guy Biederman*......................124

    Six Word Stories - *2E League Members* 125

Poetry 127

    Infinite - *Margaritë Camaj* 129

    The Cleanse 130

    Flawed 131

    Amore - *Hannah Fields*......................132

    And Still I Love You More - *Elise Holland* 134

    Love and Romance - *Michel Krug*......................135

    Mother's Day Poem 135

    Love Rhyme......................136

    I Love:......................137

    Barstools and Nightstands - *David Lukas* 139

    Window Shopping 140

    Are You Still Watching 141

    B Bar......................143

    Extra Credit......................144

Love Poem 145
A Love Letter to Me - *Francesca Lupini* 146
My Own Sun 146
Yellow Rain Boots 147
Solitary 148
Discounted Artwork 149
Dawn 150
My Favorite Color 151
Usual Desires - *Lisa St. John* 152
What I Want 152
Maybe Then 154
Peter Pan's Madrigal 156
The Whens of Now 157
There are Dreams 158
Listen 159
I am Thirsty for You 160
Crush 162
Where is Ophelia's Mother? 163

How to Submit Your Short Fiction or Poetry 164
About the 2E League 165
About the Authors 166

Labor of Love: A Letter from the Editor

WHEN YOU THINK OF a labor of love, what's the first thing that comes to mind? You might think of work done for the benefit of someone (or something) you love. Perhaps you are reminded of profound sacrifices and meaningful compromises you've made over the years in the name of a significant other or a child. Or, the idiom may initially take a different shape in your mind—in which case you might think of work done for the satisfaction of the work itself.

When I think of a labor of love many things come to mind, and the fruits of several of those labors lie right here in this book. I think of the brave and inspired work of each writer who submitted a piece of fiction or poetry to be included in this anthology. It takes creative momentum to pen a draft and polish it, and it takes courage to be willing to share that work with an editor and a community of readers. I think of those writers, and the late nights they spent with inky palms and a fickle muse, and mornings spent proofreading with coffee and conviction.

I'm extremely grateful to each writer who submitted work to be considered for this anthology, whether that piece was selected (this time) or not. To each and every one of you, I send sincere encouragement and hope you will continue to write and share your words with the world. I am also grateful to Ashly Hilst (of Ink & Grace Editing) and to Lorna and Mark

Reid (of AuthorPackages) for helping to make the dream of this anthology a reality.

When I think of a labor of love, I also think about 2 Elizabeths and what the brand and publication has meant to me personally. I think of late nights spent reviewing submissions, and the difficult decision of which stories and poems to publish either online or in this anthology. I think of the joy it has been to watch our community grow and to connect with so many of you in ways that never would have been possible otherwise.

When you read this anthology, it is my hope that you will feel the labor of love that went into creating it—not just from myself as an editor, but from each person who contributed to it. I'd like to think your copy will wind up on your coffee table, dog-eared or highlighted—evidence that you've loved the experience of reading it as much as we've loved creating it.

Elise Holland
Editor-in-Chief at 2 Elizabeths

Fiction

Making Lemonade
Catherine Brown

CONNOR FINALLY CAME CLEAN about his secret two days before our Las Vegas wedding. After our drive from Los Angeles, we stopped at a bistro for lunch. The waiter brought tall glasses of ice water garnished with lemon slices and dropped off the menus. I knew what I was going to order so I sipped my water, glad to beat the heat of the desert city. I looked across at my fiancé. Despite developing sweat stains under the arms of his yellow polo shirt, Connor didn't touch his ice water.

He glanced up from the menu and noticed I was looking at him. He frowned and ran his hand over his short blond hair.

"Cassandra, I have to tell you something."

I felt a quiver of alarm. We'd decided to elope a week ago to save money and to take advantage of a friend's timeshare in Hawaii for the honeymoon. With a dozen details that still needed to go right for our small ceremony, I wanted it to be perfect.

"What did you forget?" My mind whirled. Black socks? A tie? The tux?

"No, that's not it. I—"

With the uncanny bad timing exhibited by wait staff everywhere, our server arrived to take our order. My annoyance flared, but Connor would tell me later, and we would deal with whatever it was. I ordered the organic beets with lemon vinaigrette and the smoked salmon quinoa salad.

"My fiancé will have the same," I said. Connor always ordered exactly what I chose. It made ordering so much easier, and I enjoyed it because we could compare notes on the food.

"No, I won't," he said firmly. "I am having the steak and fries. Medium well."

I looked up in surprise, as the waiter thanked us and withdrew.

"Fries?" I asked.

"Yes, Cassandra. Fries."

"You never eat fries!"

"No, *you* never eat fries."

"But this is a perfect opportunity to try their quinoa salad. The reviews I read say it's amazing."

"I don't even know what quinoa is. I know I am not going to like it. So, I am ordering fries." Then he picked up his fork and fished the lemon slices from his glass, dumping them into mine. Confused, I digested this news about his palate. I was sure we'd had quinoa together before. Then I remembered the wedding.

"So, what were you going to tell me?"

"That I'd rather have steak and fries," he said.

"That's it?"

"Yes."

He changed the subject and talked about the activities he wanted to try in Hawaii. He was an athletic guy and he was excited about the opportunity to go windsurfing and hiking. Normally I would have chimed in, talking about the highly rated restaurants I wanted to visit, but I held back. Something wasn't right. After a few minutes, he noticed my mood and asked me what was wrong.

I'd finally put my finger on it. It wasn't just the quinoa.

"Why did you give me your lemon slices?" I asked.

"I hate lemons."

His words struck me as completely absurd. "But I love lemons!" I said. "Lemon bars, lemonade, lemon drops! I am obsessed with lemons. I love the bright tart zing in my mouth. I can't live without lemons!"

"Then don't," he said. "But I plan to."

"But—"

"Cassandra, I'm not a foodie. To be perfectly honest, I have been choking down the froufrou food that you love so much because I am crazy about you."

"Who are you, and what have you done with Connor?" I tried to joke.

He leaned forward on his elbows, his eyes level with mine. "I'm sorry, honey," he said.

"Sorry?"

"I misled you because I had some foolish idea of impressing you," he continued. "I thought maybe I would find out I liked the fancy food, and we'd have something in common. But I don't. When I saw the damned lemon slice in my water and looked at that menu, I knew I couldn't do it for the rest of my life."

"Wow." I couldn't decide how to respond. It occurred to me that I was about to marry a man I didn't entirely know.

He reached across and put a warm, strong hand on my arm. His look was beseeching.

"That's who I am, Cassandra. I love you, but I am a mac and cheese guy. A fries guy. A nachos guy. I am not a shrimp bougainvillea guy. Not a sushi prosciutto guy. Not a foie gras sangria guy."

My ears burned a little at his mangling of foodie lingo. I prided myself on my foodie credentials. I even had my own foodie blog and had a lot of followers. I had assumed that Connor was a kindred spirit in his love of food.

"Foie gras is duck liver. It doesn't go with sangria." It was reflexive, but it was all I could manage.

"In my opinion, it doesn't go with anything."

"Foie gras goes with everything!" I said, dimly registering that I'd contradicted myself.

"Foie gras is crap. I can't stand it," he said with a shrug. "But I do love you, and we can eat wherever you want. I am just the guy who will be ordering the most boring thing on the menu. I'm sorry I didn't tell you sooner."

There wasn't much I could say, so I changed the subject back to Hawaii.

After we finished, we walked back to the casino lobby to meet our friends who'd just arrived from Los Angeles. Connor kissed me and left with two buddies for some bachelor party gambling.

I paired up with my matron of honor, Evie, for some shopping. Evie was the picture of Las Vegas fun in her yellow top and bright pink capris, but her red hair looked a little flat in the heat. She dragged me up and down the strip in search of the perfect jewelry for the wedding. I welcomed the distraction for several hours.

Later, we stopped for cocktails. I ordered a lemon drop martini on the rocks. I tried to join in the chatter about our purchases, but the lemon drink made me think about Connor's words. I decided to confide in Evie and told her what had happened.

"So, he's not a foodie." She shrugged and took a sip of her mimosa.

"He isn't! He said he isn't into shrimp bougainvillea."

Evie giggled. "Ha! Bougainvillea is a plant. He must not be into gardening either. That's hilarious."

"Not as hilarious as the sushi prosciutto," I said. I stirred my drink and the ice cubes clinked. She laughed harder.

"Stop laughing," I begged. "What am I going to do?"

"Don't let him write copy for your blog," she managed with a gasp. "Oh wait, do let him write copy for your blog!" She slapped the table, all but doubled over.

"Now you're hilarious," I said, rolling my eyes. "Seriously, Evie. What am I going to do? Can I go through with this?"

She stopped laughing and looked at me. "What is this, Cassandra? Cold feet? For real?"

"I didn't think I'd get cold feet with Connor, but right now I'm barefoot with the penguins. For starters, he lied to me."

"What? About his taste in food?" She shook her head.

"Well yeah. I'm a food blogger. It's pretty important."

"Is it deal-breaker important? Are you seriously going to dump the man you've told everyone you love because he prefers fries to quinoa?"

"When you put it that way it sounds terrible," I protested.

"I think it's a crazy deal-breaker for a relationship," she countered. "Do you love him?"

I turned it around in my mind. I had known Connor for almost a year. "I thought I did. Does this mean I don't?"

"Only you can answer that, Cassandra. When did you know he was the one?"

I pondered it for a moment. Then I remembered. "I knew when he said my dog was more important than his car. Snickers wrecked the backseat when we took him to the vet." Tears welled up in my eyes when I thought about it. "Yeah, I do love Connor for that."

"That didn't have anything to do with food, did it?"

"No," I admitted.

"Connor has his priorities in the right place, from the sound of it."

"Yeah, he does," I agreed.

"Do you?"

I winced at her blunt question. "So, I'm making too big of a deal out of the food," I said. "But he should have told me."

"Did he say he was sorry for not telling you?"

"He did apologize," I said. "And he did say we could still go to the restaurants I love."

"So, you can forgive him, and we can get on with this wedding?" Evie asked.

"I suppose. But what am I going to cook at home?" When I said it, I knew I was grasping.

"Oh darn," Evie said with mock irritation. "You may just have to invest in some new recipe books to cook for your husband."

"I guess so." The idea had appeal but I wasn't ready to say so.

"And maybe you can start a feature on your blog for picky palates."

I stared at her. My mind whirled with possibilities. "Evie, you're a genius!" With my last feeble objection dealt with, I happily moved on to discussing potential blog posts.

The next morning, Connor and I walked over to the chic jewelry store in our casino hotel to purchase rings. We browsed the magnificent diamonds inside the bright cases together for a while. The rings gleamed against the clean neutral tones of the store. Then we split up to choose our favorites and I wandered over to look at the men's rings.

"Cassandra, I found your ring," Connor called out. "And it's perfect for you," he said as I walked over. "It's a lemon."

It was indeed a lemon: a gorgeous lemon diamond with a pale-yellow sparkle.

"Wow. It's beautiful," I breathed.

"Not as beautiful as the lady I am giving it to," he said. "I love you, Cassandra."

I looked at the man I was marrying, with tears in my eyes. My second thoughts from the day before died a well-deserved death.

"I love you too, Connor," I said. "And about yesterday? The food thing?"

"Yes?" he asked, with a wary expression.

"It's okay. I'm sorry you thought you had to impress me that way. It's about us, not the food. I know that now."

"I'm glad," he said, with a broad smile. "Now let's buy this ring."

"And then we can get some lunch," I said. "I am going to try some fries."

He laughed. "Let's just find some Florentine lasagna. I don't hate all the food you like, you know."

THE END

The Shoebox
R.B. Frank

IT WAS JANUARY 21ˢᵀ and no one should die so young. Jonas Welsh was not as young as some, but forty-two seemed like half a life to him. And to his family.

And all felt cheated.

Jonas knew his time was near. Conversation about the weather and what they had done that day was replaced by hushed tones, and his wife and kids took turns sitting with him. Counselors asked him questions. *What was he most proud of? Was there anything he wished he had done?* They filled in the answers for him. He couldn't see how any of that helped anyone and if they were really as compassionate as they were supposed to be, they'd just sit there and say, *Wow, this sucks* and leave it at that. But it did prompt him to remember a past hidden from all, long forgotten even by him.

When his best bud visited on what would be his final morning on earth, Jonas shooed everyone from the room and pulled his friend close.

"I want you to promise you'll do something for me. "

"Of course, whatever you need. "

"There's a box at the back of my closet. Please mail it," Jonas said. "Today."

"To where? " his friend asked.

Jonas leaned over and opened the nightstand drawer. Tucked inside a Stephen King paperback that he would never finish was a wrinkled, college-ruled slip of paper. His shaking hands pulled it out and pushed it into his friend's hand.

"Done," his friend said.

It was January 25th and Elaina McKenzie had never married. The shoebox-sized parcel was left on her doorstep, waiting for her return, getting rained on. The neighbor forgot to get the mail that day. Great. *Thanks.* She swung her backpack higher over her shoulder so it wouldn't flop and grabbed the box. She crossed the threshold, dropped her bags, and glanced at the return label. She did not recognize the name or the address but whatever. It wasn't like she was a congressional rep where she had to worry if it was anthrax.

She sunk into the couch and took a deep breath. Home smelled good. After three months in the poorest sections of Ecuador, home was comforting. And safe. Photojournalism was as exhausting as it was satisfying.

She set the package on her lap and stared at it as if she could mentally see what was inside. Finally, she pulled at the wrapping and revealed that it was, indeed, a shoebox. It was old. Really old and held together at the corners with gray duct tape. *Who would send me something like this?* She pulled at the tape that bound the top and her breath stopped. *Oh. My. God.* Her fingers riffled through a stack of letters, all addressed to her. But she had never received these letters; they were not even postmarked. These envelopes were not familiar. But the handwriting was. *Jonas.* A folded note sat on top. Her heart pounded and there was a hum in her ears as she fanned the envelopes on the couch. Elaina hesitated with the note in her hand. Her palms didn't sweat in the middle of an Ecuadorian forest but they did now.

Dear Elaina,

If you are receiving this box, most likely I'm already gone. I've been sick for the past six months with lung cancer.

No, Jonas

My life after you was full and happy, and I truly hope yours was as well. I know you never found anyone for any length of time after us. Call it stalking. But you were a thread of my life that was difficult to sever.

What you have before you is my collection. I thought it was about time I mailed these letters. For me, you were always out there, somewhere. If I wrote a letter, I felt I was still talking to you, confiding in you. And you helped me out on more than one occasion without you even knowing it. Even the decision to marry Anne. You see, it didn't matter if the letters I wrote never saw a stamp. You were there.

I understand why you broke it off. You had to travel and you loved it. I know you loved me, too. At least I hoped you did.

I did, Jo.

What I think you didn't see at the time is that the heart expands to love. You felt you had to choose. You didn't have to. I would have waited. I always would have waited. So here are the letters to you that I never mailed. There was always space in my heart for you, a corner that no one ever filled. The heart is never full.

And one final thought. Jump, my Elaina. Take that leap. Reach out if someone is there waiting.

All my love,
Jonas

Elaina sobbed for a solid hour. She recalled how she had broken it off with him because she wanted to take that two-month assignment in the Galapagos and then three months in Venezuela. She hadn't realized she didn't have to choose. Even though he said he would wait. *Idiot.* At forty years old, she now realized that she could love deeply in different ways on many levels. The folly of youth. Elaina wept over the letters and her tears turned the ink into tiny, indecipherable puddles. Her travel photos on the wall were little comfort to her now.

It was February 14th, Valentine's Day, and Elaina had a date. It was a fifth date, actually. Dinner went well and the conversation was easy. The silence was comfortable, and she judged how well a date was going if she could be in his presence and not feel as if she needed to be a camp counselor. There were very few people she had ever wanted to spend more than two hours with and this date was exceeding four. *Now for the bad news.* Over a shared dessert, she told him she was leaving next week for two months for a small village in Mumbai.

She smiled, and her eyes burned with tears when he said, "I'll wait."

THE END

The Message
James Magner, MD

THE BEST THING THAT happened to me in college was meeting Olivia Ann Evans.

Those years prepared me well for my future career as a small-town high school chemistry teacher. More importantly, being on campus allowed me the opportunity to fall in love with a college classmate, Olivia. We married two years after we graduated.

Olivia's black, curly hair and warm, brown eyes had drawn me to her as I walked into my freshman Latin class, and I took the empty seat next to her. I had chosen to take Latin because I thought it might help me later in science, whereas Olivia had taken two years of Latin in high school, so this language was a natural choice for her. It turned out that I was pretty terrible at Latin, but Olivia became a good friend. She studied with me. So, I passed.

I repaid Olivia for her language assistance by coaching her in analytic geometry. We had a running joke through the years. As she entered classrooms to sit for challenging math tests I always sent her a brief text of encouragement, "Carpe diem." Of course, this means *seize the day*. Afterwards, if she was certain that she had done well, she would text me back *omnes bene est—all is well*.

Our friendship grew into love, and I proposed marriage during junior year with the idea that we would have the ceremony after we graduated. It turned out that those plans were delayed another year by the onset of my lymphoma. But after radiation to my chest together with other treatments, the doctors seemed satisfied that I was cured. Olivia and I had little money in our checking accounts, so to celebrate my medical recovery we kept it simple—we had steaks at a local restaurant where we exchanged humorous coffee mugs. The future seemed bright, and we shortly thereafter completed the wedding plans. She made clear, however, that she would keep Evans as her last name since she didn't really care for my last name, Debreceli. She was independent-minded, and I liked her for that.

I took a job as a science teacher at an academically strong but financially struggling Catholic high school, and Olivia became an account manager at a local company.

In December I received an invitation to a science teachers' retreat. The event was to be held in mid-March on the campus of my alma mater. I showed the invitation to Olivia and I was excited that I would likely see some of my former classmates and learn how they were doing with their new teaching careers. Olivia was happy for me to go, but she had to work.

The retreat was valuable, and I also enjoyed strolling around the campus because Olivia and I had made so many memories there.

During the drive home there was little traffic at midnight on the two-lane highway in this region of farm fields. It was dark but the road was dry, good conditions for mid-March. Soon I would be crawling into a warm bed with Olivia. I was adjusting the radio when I saw a blur come at me from my left.

Wham! Suddenly I was dead.

Of course, I didn't realize it at first. It took several minutes for the notion to crystalize.

I had felt no pain. The lights came back on a second later and I found myself floating about thirty feet directly above two mangled, smoking, entangled cars. Of course, I was pretty freaked out for the first couple of minutes to find myself floating there suspended by, it seemed, an invisible cable attached to my back. I touched my face, chest, and abdomen, and all seemed normal. My skin was warm, and I had no trauma. I was wearing the same flannel shirt and old blue jeans I had put on that morning. How could I just float in the air above these wrecked cars? After about two minutes I realized that I must either be dreaming or dead, and the second option seemed more likely because I clearly had just been driving. I waved my arms and kicked my legs without effect, and I looked down at the sandals and socks on my feet.

Olivia always told me not to wear socks with sandals. "It makes you look like an old man," she had complained.

But my sandals were my most comfortable shoes. And in the cool March weather I insisted on wearing socks with my sandals. Just logical to me.

"I wouldn't be caught dead wearing sandals and socks," she had said.

Well, I had been!

I realized that I was still thinking clearly, and after the initial shock had worn off I was even finding some humor in the situation. I remained a bit nervous, but I was more optimistic that perhaps death might work out well for me. Besides, there was nothing that I could do about it. I was stuck, hanging in the air as if I were on a hook.

I looked to the left and right. No cars were yet coming along this lonely highway. The night air was cool on my face, and I could smell the earth. Stars twinkled overhead, and the familiar constellations were a comfort.

I placed my fingertips on a shirt sleeve to experience again the soft sensation of the flannel, but I noticed that the cloth now felt altered. I looked down and found that I was wearing blue and white striped pajamas. This unexpected change in my clothing was disconcerting, but within seconds I had calmed myself. The pajamas seemed familiar. Yes! These were the very same striped pajamas that Grandma Phelps had given me for my eighteenth birthday. I had loved these pajamas and had worn them through my college years until they had gotten so worn and ragged that I had to throw them out. I concluded, still scrambling to think clearly, that my clothes, and probably my body, did not exist any longer as fixed physical entities. Yet they felt normal to me.

It was only a little disconcerting when I looked at my sleeves five minutes later and I found myself back in my flannel shirt and old blue jeans. For some reason, this shape-shifting did not bother me because I knew that I was in the grips of something far beyond my understanding. I would remain calm, I decided, as long as I had no pain and could think clearly.

I looked straight down and scanned the wreckage again. A car had crashed at high speed into the driver's side of my car, nearly cutting my car in half. As I looked left and right I could see that the car must have approached on a small paved road and the driver had failed to stop at a stop sign. The idiot! The impact had caused the twisted, merged autos to slide sideways and forward off the highway, through a wire fence, and about thirty yards into the field, leaving marks in the stubble and black dirt along the trajectory. It must have been a tremendous collision.

My thoughts turned to Olivia. She would be devastated. I wondered if there were some way I could communicate to her that I was still sentient and comfortable in the next life, but that seemed highly improbable. We were Catholics, but she had been less religious. I hoped her faith would comfort her. We had no children, of course, so my next thoughts were about my students and workmates. We would miss each other. My thoughts drifted further. I wondered if I might see my parents and others who were already populating heaven.

It may seem bizarre, but I next thought about how this was March 16 and my federal and state income taxes were due on April 15. I had assembled all of the 1099 forms and statements on my desk in the living room, and I had purchased the software package but I had not yet begun completing the forms. I hoped that Olivia would easily find the statements on my desk. I felt a little guilty, but I also was happy that I would not have to struggle through that April exercise. In fact, it began to sink in that I would never again fill out income tax forms! I laughed out loud when it struck me that the topic of taxes was running through my spiritual mind twenty minutes after my death. Death and taxes, indeed.

Suddenly I saw a small flash of light to my right. The invisible cable holding me in the air started to move me toward that light, which became gradually brighter. As it grew still brighter I had to shut my eyes and I even covered them with my hands. When I next peeked out between my fingers I realized that the light intensity was normal again, and I was sitting in a chair in a small, ordinary office. At a desk in front of me was an elderly man dressed in a grey pin-striped three-piece suit, complete with white bow tie. He was typing on the keyboard of his laptop. After a moment he looked up at me.

"Mr. Stuart Debreceli, welcome to your entrance interview," he announced.

I sat in stunned silence, so he continued, "I am Saint Peter and this is, as you would say, the pearly gate. Hardly a gate though, as you can see."

"So, this is heaven?" I murmured, still a bit disoriented.

"It's just the entrance, but before you enter there are a few things to clear up," he replied as he scanned his computer screen.

As I composed myself, I looked again at his immaculate three-piece suit. "I thought that you would be wearing a white robe."

He smiled at me, and lifted his right index finger three inches from the keyboard. Instantly the three-piece suit changed to a flowing white robe. He smiled a bit more broadly as he observed my startled expression. Then he briefly lifted his finger again, and the robe changed back to a three-piece suit. "The clothes and this little office are just manifestations to make you feel more comfortable as you enter your new life."

"And you use computers in heaven?"

"Of course not!" he replied. "Centuries ago I sat here with a scroll and quill pen, then for more centuries I sat here with a thick leather-bound book. But the new fad is to use a laptop. The truth is, those things are only props and all the information is right up here." He smiled and pointed with one finger to his head.

"So," I began tentatively, "have I been approved to enter heaven?" My mouth was dry and my hands were trembling. I swallowed hard as I realized what a momentous question this was.

"Of course you have been approved! You were a loving man with acceptably strong faith and hope. So, you may now stand up and take a few steps through that door. You'll be there for all eternity, and you will find it to be superb. Congratulations, and well deserved!"

I'm sure that my relief was plainly visible. I gathered a bit more courage

"That is truly wonderful," I replied. "But may I ask a question?"

"How can I help you?"

"My young wife, Olivia Evans, will be very upset by my death. Could I briefly appear to her to tell her not to worry about me—could I tell her that I am in heaven?"

He looked me in the eyes for a few seconds, then responded. "No appearances or anything like that. In present times communications from the grave are strictly forbidden. All of that hocus pocus about mediums and ghosts is a bunch of hogwash." He paused, then added, "People on Earth must find their way to the truth without such help. It is all part of a larger plan, you see."

I was still worried about Olivia. I was afraid that she might become despondent, and perhaps even bitter. She was a strong woman, and I didn't want her to react to my death by starting an argument with God. She might come to view God as unfair and ugly. How could she respect a God who had snuffed out the young life of her good-hearted husband? After a moment I tried another approach with my host.

"If ghostly appearances are not allowed, could I perhaps leave a short letter for her to find among my things? Please understand that I am desperate to find some way to comfort and reassure her."

Saint Peter smiled knowingly at me. "No appearances, no phone calls, no vivid dreams, no letters."

My mind was racing. I had a feeling that once I walked through the door into heaven proper I might find myself with no opportunity ever to try to send a message to Olivia. Perhaps my mind might be elevated or changed in some way that I would no longer even have that concern about trying to console her. I suspected that I had to act fast.

"What if Olivia should find a little reminder of me that might console her? It would be a very general sort of thing without any concrete specific message. Could that be allowed?"

Saint Peter sighed and shrugged.

"Allowing a loved one to find or experience a remembrance can, in fact, be permitted. Your desire to console and reassure your loved one is not unique. I have had this conversation millions of times. I even have some suggestions for you. Presently the number one requested sign is to have a rainbow appear briefly after the burial. The number two request is to have a special song coincidentally play on the radio as a spouse is traveling to the funeral. Those are both acceptable signs. Of course, they are general occurrences that could be due entirely to chance, and they do not clearly communicate anything about your status in the afterlife. But either of those signs would be allowable if you would like to choose one. I can put in the order on this non-existent laptop right now if you like."

In a flash I had an idea. My heart was racing, though, because I thought that my request might not fully meet the restrictive communication criteria, and I might precipitate a scolding.

"Saint Peter, a few years ago I recovered from lymphoma. To celebrate my cure, Olivia and I exchanged coffee mugs during a steak dinner. The coffee mug that I gave her that night is sitting with her sewing stuff in the corner of the bedroom, and that cup now holds a pair of scissors and several emery boards. Would it be possible to remove the stuff from the mug, and move that mug to the center of her desk on the other side of the bedroom? She writes letters and pays bills at the desk, so she will quickly find the mug."

"A coffee mug?"

"Yes, it was a special gift from me and we had a running joke about it."

Saint Peter was amenable, but he remained a bit suspicious. "But are there slogans written on that mug? There can be no clear, concrete communication."

"No words," I replied. "Just initials." Then I continued, "And finally, it would be great to have my unopened box of income tax software placed next to that mug on her desk. She would see it as a sign that she could drink coffee and think about me as she completes our taxes."

"Just initials on the mug," Saint Peter mumbled. "Her name is Olivia Evans. Hmmm."

"Yes, there are just three letters on the mug. But she will certainly think of me when she finds it."

After a moment Saint Peter winked at me, but I was uncertain what he meant. "I actually think I am being hoodwinked here," he said. "You had better take care if you try to play tricks on beings with infinite wisdom."

I swallowed and looked down at my socks and sandals.

I looked up again and I was relieved that he was smiling. His smile, however, seemed to indicate that he knew more than he was about to say.

"Well, I will allow it in this case," Saint Peter responded with a definitive air. "You are a good man, Stuart." His fingers flew over his non-existent keyboard. Then he stood and reached out his hand. I stood and shook his hand, and then he guided me briskly through the door into heaven.

Heaven is gorgeous, but in spite of the many distractions I persisted with keeping a watch on my house. The next morning's phone call from the police with news of the accident was unbearably painful for Olivia. After she hung up the phone she sobbed in bed for an hour.

Finally, she got dressed, and sat for a moment at her little desk. I smiled as I saw her notice the mug and tax software. After a glance at the unopened software package, she set that aside. But she weighed the mug in her hand. She looked toward her sewing table then back at the mug. She walked across the room and picked up the scissors and emery boards, and after a few seconds she set them down again and returned to her desk. She looked at the mug for a full minute, seemingly without breathing.

Although my heart was already full of joy in heaven, my elation was further increased as I watched my true love murmur the initials on the mug.

"OBE," she whispered. "Omnes bene est."

Her eyes filled with tears of joy, and she fell to her knees on the carpet as she clutched the mug to her chest.

THE END

Sea Glass
Brandi Willis Schreiber

THREE COLORS BROUGHT ME to you, but only one made me stay.

I haven't seen you in years, but even before you turn toward me, the curve of your cheek pensive against the sound of my approach, I recognize that lean fold of your body in the chair, the way you absently run your fingers through the rocks where you sit.

How many times had I seen you do that: pick up some object closest to you and toss it while you talked to your friends or waited for dinner at our house? It was like you had to touch something to think, and more than once I wished it was me.

Because I couldn't bear to look at your face all those years ago, the heat creeping up my neck from those thoughts I had, I settled on your hands instead. I sketched pages of them: how your long fingers wrapped around a football before it sang like a missile through the air, how they blanched against a pencil as you bent over some homework, writing furiously in the lamplight of our den.

Later, those hands reached for girls between classes, behind chipped locker doors, in the wings of our school's auditorium where the stage's black curtains cast dark shadows. One day you caught me staring after theatre practice, your hands on some sleek midriff I don't remember, and you just gave me that shy, brotherly smile reserved for your best friend's little sister, and turned the girl into the wings, out of my sight.

Only once did I ever see those hands bloodied and bulging with veins as they clutched some rumpled shirt near the neck. The boy was trouble, a year older, and I knew to keep a wide distance. But walking the half mile home after school, I heard your shout, angry and rough, behind the fieldhouse. Pinned there against the chain-link fence, the boy kicked and hissed like an animal, but your hands were balled steel, unerring.

Later, at our house, I could only concentrate on doctoring your seeping knuckles and left the blooming bruise on your eye to you.

"He shoved Derek," you explained. "Pushed him down hard and then kicked his books across the hall." Derek, the boy who had Downs syndrome, who had been in my class as long as I could remember. Our mascot at every game and the leader of our spirit week. Your friend. The fury surged in me, and I saw it still lingered in your eyes when mine flew to yours.

"He won't be doing that again."

Your resolute expression, the mess of hair and grass across your forehead, the sense of justice vibrating from your skin. It was all too much. I left you at the kitchen table. And I knew that with graduation, you would do the leaving next.

I was right. For a while, we sang our pleasant song as life in our small town turned over and the years faded like seafoam into one another. Then commencement came, and with it, your body—taller, leaner, folded into the musty chairs of our auditorium—and your profile, strong against the sun as my mother snapped photos and wept.

You did leave.

But before you did, your dented Ford packed to overflowing and idling in our driveway, you pulled me to you while my brother soothed our parents on the lawn. It was the only time you'd ever touched me, and I became stone. You held me to your chest, waited for my body to relax. I forgot what arms should do, forgot my own breath while you rested your chin against my head. You sighed—the sound much too old—and gripped my shoulders so you could look at me. Without saying a word, you kissed my forehead and climbed into your truck, throwing goodbyes out the window until the very end.

I knew you would save the world.

I just didn't realize until that moment you'd never come back to save mine.

***

That was twelve years ago.

And now, on this hot beach tumbling in a rough cliff to sea, here are those hands again, those long fingers grazing the pebbles. Ten yards away, and I know it's you, my primitive lower brain kicking into gear at the familiar pattern.

I want to stop and go back to the car. But I've come to this beach from San Juan, where a shopkeeper told me I'd find three colors in the sand, and I can't stop my descent. I skid down the embankment, sending stones ahead of me, and you turn at the sound.

Only it isn't you. At least not all of you. Your body is tense, the side of your face tight beneath your sunglasses, a corner of your mouth unnaturally upturned as if hooked to invisible wire. I think of the rumors I've heard, how you disappeared into Sartana and Pisky and other war-torn cities after college, your byline beneath black-and-white stories rife with loss. There was an explosion, someone said, a fire, and your name stopped appearing online.

You lean out of a flimsy plastic chair, don't fully turn.

"Who's there?" It's your voice, although rough with uncertainty, like the ocean rushing toward us on this remote western island. The sound crashes over me harder than the waves and I shiver. Those hands clutch the edge of the chair like a buoy in deep water.

"Liam? It's me. Addie Lowell."

"Addie?"

You turn now to face me, your dark, oversized sunglasses hiding most of what's beneath. You're leaner than I remember, too many shadows cast beneath your cheeks and in the hollows of your collarbone. A dangerous sunburn is laid down over your bare skin, but there is still muscle in your arms and definition along your ribs where a scribble of scar tissue crisscrosses down your side. The pattern disappears beneath the band of your swim shorts, and I blush at that juncture, hoping you don't notice.

"Addie Lowell? *Ho-ly hell*. What are you doing in Rincón?"

"I came to find sea glass."

You don't scoff at my bizarre answer, just lean back against your chair, the good side of your mouth hitched in a small smile.

"Of course you are. Who else would come all the way to Puerto Rico to find sea glass?"

And there is that old familiarity, the boy who is in every corner of my childhood. I start toward you and then remember this is you, and this is a beach, and I've come here in a bathing suit during the low season when the waves are too unpredictable for the surfers and the heat too oppressive for the tourists. No one else is supposed to be here, least of all you.

The distance hangs between us. Twelve years hang between us, too. Years of work and wreckage, unobtrusive holidays back home, and life lived in small measures in the in-between. And of nothing of significance except the memory of your chin pressed against my hair and your hands on my shoulders.

I pull my towel around me in a makeshift skirt and sit down next to you. You don't look at me, don't even evaluate me for a second. You just turn back toward the lucid horizon, your hands paling in their grip against the plastic.

"Addie Lowell in Puerto Rico," you murmur. "On the same beach as me. Jesus H. Christ, what are the odds? What has it been, Addie?" you whisper. "Twelve years?"

"Since you left Endsland? Yeah."

A muscle in your neck quivers, and I sense you reaching for something. "I thought I'd go back someday and see your folks, Addie. And you." This last part you say with a quick incline of your head toward me. "But it just never worked out to make the trip home. I sure didn't want to see my old man."

I think about your dad, always rumpled and greasy and a little too jerky, observing us from a suspicious distance whenever we were at baseball games or town holidays. If other rumors are true, he had a drinking problem. I wonder if he had a problem with you, too.

"How is your brother?"

It didn't occur to me you might not know about my brother, your best friend from high school and college roommate. "He's married now, living near Georgetown. They have a baby. I just got back from seeing them a few weeks ago."

Your exhale rushes out as if you've been holding a long breath. "Good. I'm glad. I'm happy for him. And . . . you?" You cast a glance at me, look away again. "Your folks?"

"I'm still there in Endlands with them. I have been since college." But the words are bitter. "What are you doing in Puerto Rico?"

"I live here now." Without turning, you point above us, and I notice a thick length of rope hemming makeshift stairs leading up the escarpment to a handful of houses above, spaced like colorful dominoes along the cliff ledge.

"And do what?" I ask.

"Online consulting for travel, mostly. Some freelance work for a few newspapers. PR is a good place to do that. All you need is a computer and the internet. A lot of expats with virtual careers live here. Writers, artists. You would like it."

You try to smile, but I hear disappointment in your voice, so I look out to sea where your gaze has been steady. In the overhead sun, the water is aqua and white-frothed, lapping impatiently at the rocky beach. In a few hours, the horizon will be swathed in pink and orange fire before it melts into black glass, smeared and dotted with the stars of other worlds. I've seen this light the two nights I spent in San Juan, and it took my breath away. Yes, I do like Puerto Rico. I glance back at the houses above me. From where you live, it must be such a view.

But it's a view you never told my brother about, never shared with anyone back home. You disappeared from us and left us to wonder why.

"You were a war correspondent." I say the words slowly, and you tip your head toward me. "I read all your pieces. You went to Syria, the Ukraine. I followed your work online, saw all the photos you took. You scared the shit out of us, Liam."

You remain quiet a moment. "Someone had to do it, Addie. Someone had to write about what was happening, talk about how people were suffering. And I knew I could do it. So, I went."

And there you've done it: You've rushed headlong into the heart of it, the same way you rushed onto the field, into the foolish confidence of young girls' arms, into the borderlands from which people never returned. But your response is a scrape against an old wound.

"You nearly died doing it, though. And now you're here, in Puerto Rico? Why haven't you told us where you've been? Why haven't you come back to South Carolina?"

You don't answer me. You won't even look at me.

I stand and walk toward the water.

***

In 1899, bound for Savannah, a merchant steamer slammed into the coast near Port Royal Sound, spilling its contents into the frigid water. Among other things, the ship was supposed to deliver furniture and tins tight with fish. But the white ice sheared the waters into slim knives, and its iron hull crashed against the shoals. Chairs, leather shoes, medicinal bottles poured out of its side in a brown bloodlet as the men screamed and fought to reach the sand.

For years, islanders hauled into their houses what washed ashore: beaten side tables and half-toys. But the shards of South Carolina Dispensary bottles rolled in and out with the tides, unclaimed.

Nearly 120 years later, deep in a South Carolina cove, with my brother's baby on my hip and the rest of a picnic abandoned to the ants, I found a piece of glass, tumbled smooth, the lip of a palmetto frond still visible on one side. It shouldn't have been there. It shouldn't have survived through the hurricanes and erosion.

Where was it caught for so long before it was expelled back to sea? An inlet of thick reeds? Some windowsill before it was tossed like second trash?

I ran my finger over the swell of glass, solid but etched by salt.

Broken but still recognizable.

***

I feel you before I hear you over the crashing waves.

"Why sea glass?" Your voice is full of apology because we both know it's the wrong *why*. I look into the water where it rushes around jagged rocks, so unlike our shores back home.

You wait with a reporter's patience, and I finally give.

"It's a beautiful material to work with. And inexpensive, if you live near a place where you can find it. There are lots of types of sea glass, too. White or clear is the most common because that's the type of glass most things are packaged in. Next would probably be green, you know, made from soda bottles. But I look for the rarer colors. Blue, lavender, red."

"Have you found any?" you ask.

"A bit. But not nearly as much as I'd like."

"Is that why you're in Puerto Rico? To find the rarer colors?"

"Yeah. I heard good things about PR, and it was cheap to fly here from Charleston."

"And what do you do with this sea glass when you find it?" You sound genuinely intrigued.

"I clean it up. Polish it. Make it into jewelry or a mosaic. Sometimes a custom piece for a client." I think of my dusty shop set in the white relief of other dusty shops on our old Main Street where oily townsfolk look but rarely buy.

"I knew it." You sound vindicated.

"Knew what?"

"You always were an artist. Always watching, observing, thinking. And then running off to do something with what you saw. I remember you used to take those big pads of paper, you know the ones with the wire rings? And you'd sit in some corner and draw for hours. You'd never look up." Despite the brutal sun which has my skin prickling, I blush. So you watched me, too, then, maybe more intimately than all the other men I've known in my life.

"Yeah, well, I didn't really do much with it. I went back to Endsland after art school and have been there ever since."

"Why?"

How do I tell you I came home for you? That not knowing where you were one day to the next, if you were safe, if you were even alive, kept me scouring the web for your name? How do I say I couldn't bear the thought of you finally coming back home and me not being there, waiting across the threshold of my parent's old house? That I knew if you came back, it would be for my brother, for my parents, but I wanted to be there anyway, even knowing I was just a shadow in the room? How do I tell you I waited for you through my mother's illness and my brother's eventual move, and then, when your name disappeared and I didn't know where I could find you, I assembled my small life in the only place where I knew you might find *me*?

"It's home," is all I can manage.

You extend your hand. "Let's go find your sea glass, Addie."

I pause. This would be the second time you've touched me, but this time I refuse to freeze. With deliberate concentration, I put my hand in yours. Those fingers—warm, adept—wrap around mine.

"Lead me down to the water." Your voice is as soft as seagrass underfoot.

For a heartbeat I think it's silly guiding you when this is your beach and you know the shoreline better than me. I sweep my eyes over the riot that is the water, the rocks, the sky. "Lead *you*?"

But then it hits me: the tilt of your head, your indifferent gaze, the oversized sunglasses hiding half your face. A sharp pain lances my chest.

"Liam?"

You flinch. "You didn't know? I'm blind. Well, mostly. I can't see at all out of my right eye, and my left is pretty shot. Shapes—" you wave at the horizon with your free hand "—and light and shadow, but not the colors I used to see. If we're going to search for sea glass, you have to show me where to go. I can't . . . I can't find it for you."

A wave of blue retreats. I glance back at your flimsy plastic chair, sunk deep in the sand from your weight, and the rope that leads to your home. The small, worn things that tell you where you are, but give you nothing of the brilliant hues on this island. My throat constricts.

"I'm sorry."

You shrug as if it was a grocery list you've lost and not your sight. "Take me to the water," you say.

I navigate us around rough boulders, yellowed palm fronds, the upchuck of sea refuse on the beach. The sand is still rocky here, but I can already see the milky glint of glass in the surf. At this western point of Puerto Rico, the currents smash debris into rocks before rushing around to the northern shores where cruise ships and pretty hotels line calmer waters. But here, the first point of contact, the sea and land are wild.

"Do you see any?" you ask.

"Yes, so much." So much my eyes won't still. Glass gleams like stars beneath the water. I feel like a kid scanning a new crayon box, possibilities filling my mind.

You chuckle. "Show me."

I dip our conjoined hands into the water and free a shard from between the rocks.

"It's green." I put it in your hand, move your fingers over it. "Sort of a muted hue, like unripe limes. Feel this edge? This is probably from the lip of a bottle, like Sprite. Or maybe that awful Mountain Dew you chugged as a kid." I watch as you run your finger around the smooth ridges, imagining it whole.

"I never knew all this was here." Your voice is thick with a bit of wonder.

"Yes, it's everywhere." I reach down for a pebble of similar size, place it in your other hand. "Do you feel how the weight is different? And even the texture? If it feels grainy, that's the oxidation of the glass in the water. It sort of dissolves over time. This is how you'll know when you're feeling the rocks with your fingers, which is glass and which is just stone."

You incline your head toward me. "You see everything, don't you?" And I don't know if you're talking about now or the past. "Show me more," you say.

I inch us further into the water, time myself against the crashing waves, and free more pieces. When I find a particularly interesting shape and squeal, you laugh and pocket the glass in your shorts, the gesture warming me with its domesticity. We make our way along the shore like this, holding hands as I guide us against the rough waters, and talking of glass and whatever else we find. You know this island well, I learn: its birds and their desperate calls, the smell of an approaching storm. Even the air, you say, tastes different throughout the day.

The water has begun to slap at my knees, and you tug me to higher ground. "The tide is coming in. We should get back."

"One more piece to end our hunt." You laugh because your shorts are already slung low on your hips, the pockets heavy. I've glanced there, unabashed, many times this afternoon.

"Okay," you concede.

And with an outgoing rush of water, I see it: heart red reflected in the waves, a few feet below.

"I think I see a red piece. Hold on."

"Addie—" you protest, but I've already released your hand and jumped into the water to beat the next wave. "Dammit, be careful!" By now, the water is to my waist, and I use my foot to free the glass, cursing when a jetty swirls sand and pebble over it again.

"I'm fine! I just—" But my words are swallowed by the force of what hits me and sucks me down. Like a magnet, my body lifts and slides from the edge of the shore. I fight beneath the water, feel my fingers scrape against the rock and sand I can't grasp, and then I'm flipped over. For one brief moment I imagine my bones smashed on the rocks and scattered within my skin, and I kick. When I surface, I hear you screaming my name, your hands outstretched in the wrong direction, toward emptiness.

"Liam!" I fight the waves, pumping my legs toward shore.

You are in the water and grab for me, hauling me against you when I am close enough to grasp your body. As I sputter, I can see the fury and fear in your face, your sunglasses gone, a thick weave of scar tissue coursing across one eye and down your cheek. You pull me onto the beach. We collapse in a heaving mass.

Your pockets are empty, the sea glass washed out. Only then do I see how far down the beach we are from the frayed rope leading to your cliffs and am shamed by the distance and how you plummeted, yet again, into what you could not see.

***

After the beach, the fear and sun making us sickly, you insist on showers and food and lead me up the stairs to your house. It sleeps between two large *flamboyanes*, their flaming blossoms pulsing like blood in the cross-breezes. In the cooling evening, the air moves through your open windows like silk, and I shudder when it hits my damp skin, fresh with the plain soap you use.

In fact, everything in your home is plain. The rooms are small and uncluttered, the furniture solid and unadorned. No photos cling to walls, no books shoved into corners. Except for an office I glimpse with two blinking computer screens, it's as if you don't live here at all.

"How long, Liam?"

You maneuver through the kitchen, gathering bread and cheese, sliced mangos chilling in a lilac bowl. You've showered, too, and a masculine clean scent swamps my senses when you lean over me for plates, the bad side of your face averted.

"How long what?"

"How long have you been alone here?"

You still, but a muscle moves in your jaw.

"Five years."

"*Five*—" but I can't finish my question. Shame laces your face.

I move in, don't ask—just bring my hand to your chin and turn your head gently toward me. The right side of your face is a mesh of thick scars cascading from hairline to lip, over your brow and right eye, which is sealed like a bricked-over window. Your other eye is open. I draw my fingers down the scars splayed like rivulets and linger at your lips. You inhale sharply. Your good eye searches me, trying to make out my shape in the evening's retreating light. When you can't, you just close your eye.

"How did it happen?" I ask.

"In a village in Syria. Near Damascus. I was working on a refugee piece and interviewing people fleeing toward Lebanon. It's funny. There weren't even reports of violence in that town. At least not yet. But the hotel we were staying at came under attack. By whom, or why, we still don't know. Not a lot made sense during that time. Someone set fire to the doors."

My fingers stop. "With you inside?"

You nod. "They locked us in."

I think of the flames, the screams, the wild panic so far away from the gently lapping water below us.

"How did you get out?"

"An alley terrace on the second floor. I used to go out there at night and smoke with the cook. We could see the stars when the electricity went off, which happened often."

I think now of the melting glass around you, the smell of carpet and film burning, the jump to the ground below.

"Were there many of you?"

"Only a few, thank God."

I almost don't want to ask, but I do. "And you all got out?"

"I was the last. By then, everything was on fire, including me. The last thing I remember was leaping, and then I woke up in a hospital in Beirut."

It suddenly seems so foolish: an empty shop back home which no one visits, chunks of broken glass milky in the dirt and water.

"Addie, what is it?"

"What you did, Liam. It mattered. I don't even want to know how many times you risked your life to help people, tell people. And what I do . . ." I let the thought trail away like my hand from your face.

"Hey, art is important." You grab my hand again. "I was making my own in a way, until this." You gesture at your body. "What you create, how it affects people, however small, is lasting. I saw more than just hotels and people burn, Addie. People in that region lost everything: freedom, but also their heritage, the ability to make the art they want, freely, without fear. Their joy." You are the one to touch my face this time, a light brush, your fingers lingering at my nape. "It's not insignificant if you remember that. Make use of it." Your smile is faint, pained.

"Is that what you're doing here, Liam? Making use of it?" This close the warmth of your body pushes against mine.

"What?" You haven't yet released your touch, haven't moved your thumb from my cheek, and I feel like I'm tethered to a rocking pier.

"Are you really *living* here? In Puerto Rico? In Rincón?"

"In a way." The words, like your expression, are tight.

"But you're not happy, Liam. I know that. I can *feel* it. You've isolated yourself on purpose, so far away from everyone who loves you." And the distance between here and home, between you and not you, feels like starlight. I know if I leave your side a hundred years will pass before I see your light again. I cannot bear it, so I ask again, "Why didn't you come back?"

You wrap your arms around me and pull me to you, and the light brightens and shifts until I'm 15 and standing in my driveway again, and you're whole and young and pulsing with purpose. The smell of your skin and my mother's detergent mingle as I close my eyes against the onslaught of you. I tell the girl you're holding—the one who will later run to her room and tremble and cry for days, the one who will scan faces in the papers and cities, looking for your likeness for years, the one who will go to bed with only a handful of men and cry out your name when they enter her—to speak up, say something to the beautiful boy she's loved all her life.

Hurry, Addie. Before his hands slide away from you. Before he gets in his truck and rushes toward smoke and flame and his own death. *Say it.*

But I can't because that girl is gone, and the years are gone, and even that boy as he backs away from her, the rising sun framing his face with his long leaving, is gone.

I don't know I've been sobbing, my body shaking with grief, or that you've been repeating my name like a mantra until you push me away from you and shake me.

"Addie!"

"I'm sorry, Liam. *I'm sorry!*"

"Christ, for what?" You run your hands over my head, my face, the back of my neck, scanning for some injury.

"I let you leave. I never should have let you leave, Liam. I'm so sorry." The tears won't stop. "I should have run after you. Told you I loved you. You left and you never knew. You never knew, Liam! And you almost died. Please forgive me. God, I'm so sorry."

"Oh, Addie," you say, clutching my face with those hands. "I knew you loved me. You didn't think I knew that? I didn't need you to say it to know it. But I also knew I couldn't stay, and that's not your fault." At *couldn't stay* I feel a wave of pain again, but you won't let me buckle.

"Addie." You hold me up with the strength of your arms and put your forehead against mine to force my attention. "What could I offer my best friend's little sister? In Endsland, of all places? I had to go and make something of myself. I couldn't end up like my dad, drunk and depressed with no outlet for his rage except his fists on his son. Don't you understand? I had to leave Endsland. It was the only way I could *survive*."

I do understand. Because I left it too. But I see now it wasn't love that brought me back to its empty streets, curving out of the dank mist, or even the belief that you would come back. It was fear.

"I love you, Addie."

Your words sound far off, like a refrain caught against the wind. "What?"

This you whisper: "You didn't know I loved you too? All my life? Why do you think I was always at your house?" The shy smile returns and just as quickly evaporates. "It tore my heart out when I left. But I was 18. You were 15. I thought your brother would kill me if I ever told him, so I tried to put you out of my head, focus on girls in my grade. It never really worked. And then I had this chance to go to college, to make something of myself."

Panic surges. "Why didn't you tell me, then? Why didn't you come *back*?"

Your voice breaks. "Because I was a coward! And life happened, Addie. School, then work, then a chance to go overseas. I convinced myself I was doing the right thing. Your brother didn't want me to go. We had a huge falling out over it. He told me I was a selfish bastard, but I went anyway. And then *this* happened." I know you are talking about your body, the strained pull of skin, the shadows you can barely see. "I didn't want you to see me like this. Or anybody else from Endsland. Some burned up, washed up version of me. God, what I would give for your last memory of me to be what I was before."

"No." I shake my head violently. "No, Liam. I don't want memories. I have lots and lots of memories. I'm *sick* of memories. I don't care about your scars or your eyes, or whatever happened to bring you here. The only thing I care about is that you're okay. You're alive."

"Addie," you say, your voice thick with emotion. "After everything that's happened, I don't know I deserve that."

I think of the South Carolina Dispensary glass, the years it spent lost in sand and sea. How it waited, tangled in the seaweed and sand, until I found it.

We survived years too.

"Of course you deserve it, Liam. Just because the glass is broken doesn't make it any less valuable. You can rebuild broken relationships too. My family will understand. So will my brother. Talk to them."

"And you?" You quake. "Can you forgive me? For not . . . for being brave for everyone except you?"

Can I forgive myself? For the words I never told you, the years I spent grieving a love I never lost?

"There's nothing to forgive— "

But my words are swallowed by the hunger of your kiss. Again, you pull me against you, all of you. The soft, patient boy is gone and the one who works my mouth is starved. I can feel your desperation, the years of hollow loneliness beneath all that strength. I know it because it is mine.

Something breaks within, and we're against the counter, and suddenly the distance between years and oceans is too far. We mold to each other, grab for each other, trying to find the places on our bodies where we can hold onto time. Your hands roam over all of me, as if trying to figure out my shape. And then they slide over my shoulders to the weight of my breasts. Outside, a *coquí* gives its sweet, piercing call.

"*Addie.*"

Those hands, those fingers. Touching as if to think. But I can't think because they're on my bare skin beneath your borrowed shirt. They trail, linger.

And then you find the rest of me, and I gasp. You still again, pant against my mouth. For a second I think you might stop this, remembering your old friend, his little sister. But with a controlled strength, you breathe, "Bedroom."

We laugh like teenagers as we tumble through the doorway and fall onto your bed. The silver light through the window illuminates your long form as you pull the rest of the clothes from our bodies. It's only when I'm free of them and reaching for you that I see it: the only piece of art in your home, hung in a weather-battered frame near the door. I know those hands, those lines. I know the shipwrecked girl who drew them.

"Liam, that sketch. Where did you get that?"

The words are work, for you let the weight of your body settle over me and thread those same fingers through my hair. "Well." You look sheepish. "I stole it."

"What are you talking about?"

"I . . . took it from one of your sketchbooks when you weren't looking. You were always drawing, always somewhere else. And I—" You dip your head toward mine. "I wanted something to remember you by. So I ripped it out before I left and took it with me."

Even in the moonlight I can see the paper's frayed lines, as if folded into pocket-sized squares many times over.

"You kept it all this time?" I search your open eye, the rich amber I still remember from so long ago. The most precious color I will ever find.

You kiss me—a slow, warm wave.

"I held on to you, too, Addie. You were with me everywhere I went."

And with the surf rushing toward us below, again and again, we find each other, and revel in what we could not see, did not know was there, until we both closed our eyes and leapt.

THE END

The Triple Lutz
K.D. Van Brunt

"**M**OM!"

My sixteen-year-old daughter, Hayley, startles me, causing my fingers to slip off the laces of my ice skates.

"Guess what?"

"Hayley, you're late. Get suited up. Lessons start in ten minutes."

She responds by thrusting a copy of the local newspaper at my face and shaking it, as if I can read text while it's in motion. "Zeke Smith isn't just coming to Drayton Corners," she says. "He's coming *here*. He's doing a special demonstration at our rink. Oh my God! You *do* realize he's a freaking movie star?"

Sighing, I exhale slowly at the sight of Hayley bouncing on the balls of her feet with excitement. In stark contrast, anxiety and dread roil my stomach. The illustrious Zeke Smith is going to be the grand marshal for our town's annual fall festival and, as mayor for the day, cut the ribbon for our new recreational center. Zeke. It's hard to think of him as Zeke. When I knew him, he was David.

"I know, Hay. I talked to his manager. Unfortunately, we can't charge admission. We'll have to rely on concessions to make some money."

Hayley rolls her eyes and shakes her head in dismay. "Mom, who gives a crap about making money? Think of the publicity. Besides, it's Zeke Smith. This is *so* monumental."

"*You* need to give a crap," I retort, more sharply than I intended. "We live and die by what this fifty-year-old rink makes."

Recently, we've barely scraped by and I need Hayley. We can't afford to hire someone to take her place, so I rely on her free help with skating lessons and other odd jobs to keep our heads above water. I just need to get through a few more years, see her through college, and then I can sell the place and . . . and what? No idea.

Hayley ignores me. She's busy rereading the article. The story is full of biographical details about the illustrious Olympic-gold-medalist pairs skater, including, most prominently, the fact that he was born and grew up right here in little old Drayton Corners, just south of Madison, Wisconsin. It details all his glittery accomplishments—he's won bronze and gold medals at the Olympics, he's a TV commentator, he's a movie star, he's been married three times, and, of course, he won *Dancing with the Stars* last season. No question, Zeke Smith is a rock star. Thankfully, the piece doesn't mention his early career; it doesn't mention me.

"Mom, it says he was in the class of '96 at Drayton," Hayley notes. "Wasn't that your class?"

"Nope. I was '97."

"Did you know him?"

I can't help barking out a short laugh. "You think Drayton High is small now. You should have seen it twenty years ago. Everybody knew everybody. Yes, I knew him." Then I add quietly, almost to myself, "But he wasn't a friend."

This is the truth. David Ezekiel Smith wasn't a friend. He was much more than a friend.

"Maybe I'll get to meet him."

I shake my head. "Not likely. He's flying in the night before and flying out the next afternoon. It's all part of a promotional blitz for his upcoming movie."

Hayley and I spend the rest of Saturday morning on the ice teaching classes in basic figure skating—I teach basics level four, Hayley has basics level one. By lunchtime, we're both cold, exhausted, and drenched in sweat.

"How's your afternoon?" I ask.

She gives me a weary smile. "Two private lessons and then hockey practice."

"I'll be in the office if you need me."

After an hour battling bills and order forms, a knock on my office door distracts me from sorting through the invoices I'm reviewing.

"Come in," I holler.

When the door swings open, Drayton Corners' mayor, Sydney Trusk, stands in the entryway, and before I can say anything, she waggles her index finger at me accusingly.

"Finley," she says, "I don't understand you."

"Hello to you too, Mrs. Mayor."

"Marcus Kincaid is a great guy. You would see this if you'd just give him a chance."

With my hands clasped behind my head, I lean back in my chair and shoot her an annoyed frown.

"Syd, stop setting me up on dates. I don't have time. It's nothing personal against Marcus, but there aren't enough minutes in the day for guys, okay?"

"Wait until you're old like me, sweetie." She pastes on her grieved grandmother face. "You'll regret not taking the time to enjoy the scenery while you still have your looks."

"Warning noted."

Sydney claps her hands, which she does when she's about to the change the subject.

"About Mr. Smith," she begins. "As you know, I'm supposed to welcome him to our town when he arrives this Friday."

At the words *supposed to* I feel an ulcer coming on.

"Well, I can't," she continues. "I have a damn kidney stone, pardon my language. Doc says it has to come out now— Thursday, actually. So, you're taking my place."

"Absolutely not. Get Sue or George to do it. I don't have the temperament."

Sydney puts up her hands in a defensive gesture. "George will be out of town on business, and Sue has the disposition of a snapping turtle. Besides, we need someone youthful to represent Drayton Corners."

I can't help scowling. "Syd, I'm thirty-five—not exactly youthful."

She shushes me. "Fine. Bring Hayley. Listen, all you have to do is meet him when he arrives at his hotel, show him some town love, and then sit with him during the parade. As my granddaughters always say—easy, peasy."

So, six days later, at five o'clock, Hayley and I are standing in the lobby of the Concourse Hotel in downtown Madison, waiting with Zeke Smith's manager, Tony Bixler, for his royal highness to arrive from the airport. *Why am I here? I hate this . . . and I hate my clothes.* I'm wearing a gray wool jacket and skirt—the outfit I wear to common council meetings and when I visit my bank to renegotiate our loan. Hayley has on a navy-blue skater skirt and a long-sleeve, vanilla-colored blouse which highlights her reddish-brown hair. She's a perfect cross between my flaming red hair and her father's chestnut brown locks.

"He's a half hour late," I mutter to Hayley. "Maybe we should get his cell number and text him a welcome."

Could he be a no-show? Just as I get my hopes up, they're dashed when a babble of shouting voices erupts. I don't see Zeke Smith, but this has to be him and his entourage, since camera flashes pop and people milling about the lobby move to crowd the door. Then I spot a mop of blond hair on a guy with mirrored sunglasses at the center of things, flanked on one side by a mousy looking young girl holding an iPad—his personal assistant I'm guessing. Two TV cameramen trail behind him.

So, this is Zeke. He's wearing a Lakers sweatshirt, faded jeans, and sandals—definitely not local. The temperature is in the mid-twenties outside, so his footwear choice is a little baffling.

Hayley grips my arm tightly with a wide, excited grin. Zeke shakes hands with Tony, who takes him by the elbow and guides him toward us. Zeke has an utterly fake, plastic smile on his face as he approaches us, but then he notices me and cocks his head to one side as if puzzled. His smile evaporates, and he halts a few feet away as recognition spreads over his face and my spine suddenly tingles. I haven't seen him in person since before Hayley was born.

"Zeke," Tony says, "this is—"

"Fin?" Zeke interrupts. "Fin Dean?"

"Hello, David," I answer quietly. My voice is small and timid.

Hayley's grin vanishes, and she glances over at me, stunned that Zeke Smith knows my name.

"My God!" he gasps, pushing his shades up onto his head, revealing his glacier blue eyes. "It *is* you."

I extend my hand to shake his, but he wraps me in a crushing hug. Holding out my arms spread-eagled, I'm unable to breathe. Flashes from the photographers explode like artillery on the battlefield.

Next to me Hayley sarcastically whispers, "No, he's not a friend at all."

David glances at Hayley. "Fin and . . ." He pauses, points at Hayley, and looks questioningly at me.

"David, this is my daughter, Hayley Dean-Richter. Hayley, this is David Smith."

Hayley recovers and her grin is back as she enthusiastically shakes hands.

"I'm going to catch up with Fin for a few minutes," David tells Tony. "Push back dinner." Tony gives him several *of-course* nods.

"No need," I say. "We just wanted to welcome you back home on behalf of Drayton Corners and express our gratitude for your spending the day in our town tomorrow. And—"

"Nonsense," he interrupts. "Come on. Let's get drinks and sit for a while."

He takes me by the elbow and tugs me toward a lounge area, triggering another artillery round of camera flashes. He's pulling me along like a horse by the reins, so I gently twist my arm free and walk alongside him. A decidedly star-struck Hayley follows.

Inside the dimly lit hotel bar, we sit on pillowy, leather chairs spaced evenly around a square, wooden coffee table.

Even in the dim light I notice the sparkly stuff on his skin. He's wearing makeup.

"You look terrific, Fin," he says. "You could still fit into your junior prom dress. Remember that night?" Then he actually winks at me. He has the cordial, glad-handed demeanor of a used car salesman.

Hayley takes this all in and proceeds to stare questioningly at me with one eyebrow arched, as if expecting a confession.

"I still skate every day," I reply. "It keeps me in shape. And before I forget, thanks for holding your skating demonstration in our rink. We really appreciate it."

His eyes narrow in confusion before he clears his throat. "Your rink? You bought the old Richter Rink?"

I blink stupidly in response and clear my throat. "Ah, no, not exactly. You remember Jonas Richter?"

He nods. "How could I forget—what a dick."

Hayley's mouth falls open and her eyes widen in shock. Then she coughs politely, and an awkward moment of silence follows.

Right. How to say this.

"I married Jonas, actually. He died when Hayley was four, and the rink passed to me."

David's face turns scarlet red and he winces in embarrassment. "Did I actually say dick? Sorry. On set, this is where the director yells 'cut' and then calls me an airhead for blowing my lines again." He glances back and forth at the two of us, searching for a reaction.

Hayley busts out laughing, which causes me to smile too. No disrespect to my late husband, but I remember the way he and David bickered constantly about everything—back when David was a nobody like the rest of us.

"Shouldn't be surprised," David adds. "He always had a crush on you. So, Fin, what have I missed the last twenty years in Drayton Corners?"

I catch David up on the events in our town since he left, which doesn't take long. In Drayton Corners, the script is you grow up, you leave, and you don't come back—unless you're stuck here . . . like me. He listens patiently, but his mind seems elsewhere, and his eyes roam around not meeting mine. He's bored. Can I blame him? After a few minutes Tony interrupts us, whispering something in David's ear, who nods and rises.

"I have to take care of a small crisis," he announces. "Say, let's have breakfast tomorrow before this parade thing."

"Great!" Hayley blurts out.

"We can't," I say. "Hayley and I teach classes at the rink, starting at eight a.m. sharp."

Thank God for the classes. I don't want to have breakfast with movie star Zeke. The David I knew doesn't exist anymore, and this Zeke-the-Sleek feels about as genuine as a part-time mall Santa.

"That was interesting," Hayley observes once we're back in our car. "He kept staring at your . . . " She pauses, searching for a diplomatic phrase. "Your anatomy."

"Stop. He did not."

She snorts a laugh. "He was totally checking out your rack, Mom."

The next morning at seven, when Hayley and I pull up to the rink in our modest 2009 Toyota Corolla to unlock the doors, flick on the lights, and turn up the heat before the day begins, we find an odd sight. A shiny, blue Cadillac Escalade sits next to the handicap spaces, idling. When we emerge from our car and approach the front doors of the rink, the passenger door of the Escalade opens and David steps out, holding a drink carrier and a Starbucks bag.

"Stalker much?" Hayley mutters to me.

"Since you couldn't come to breakfast," David announces, "breakfast comes to you."

He cheerfully follows us around while we go about opening up the rink. I pass for now on the blueberry muffin he offers, but gladly accept the coffee. Usually I don't get my first Saturday morning caffeine until a break between classes, when Gus has gotten the concession stand up and running.

"So, you're subbing for the mayor today?" David asks.

"Yep, she's in the hospital and I'm her official pinch hitter."

Hayley and I wear the same outfit—the Richter Rink uniform: black leggings and a pink leotard. We don't get a lot guys at our girls' figure skating lessons, so maybe that's why my cheeks heat a little when I take my jacket off and collapse onto the floor to begin my stretches. Zeke plops down next to me, sitting cross-legged and invading my space. When his knee touches my hip, I can't help flinching. Zeke looks normal this morning: no makeup, no shades, and no entourage. And instead of California grunge, he's wearing a pressed pair of khaki slacks and a thermal T-shirt.

"I'm surprised you hung around this town, Fin. You always wanted to leave, go to college or something."

How to respond. Should I go with superficial or honest? The latter, I think.

"Well, things changed. Jonas and I married right out of high school, and we had Hayley when I was nineteen." I glance over at him, wondering if this is explanation enough, but he gives me an and-then-what-happened expression. "Jonas's parents offered to let us take over the rink, which was too good an opportunity to refuse, so we hung around."

"You ever wish you'd left?"

"Ever wish you'd stayed?"

"Yeah, I do sometimes."

I laugh out loud at this and fall back into my old slang name for him. "Give me a break, Smitty. You love being an A-lister. Admit it."

"It has its moments," he acknowledges with a smile. "So, Hayley's a figure skater too?"

"Hay grew up on the ice. She's one of the best figure skaters I've ever seen. She could skate competitively if she wanted, but her chosen sport is hockey."

"Hockey? Sacrilege."

I grin back at him. "I know, but she's even better at hockey than figure skating. Several programs have scouted her. We're hoping for some scholarship offers next year."

"You remarried?" he asks.

"Nah. Once was enough for me. How about you?"

He smirks at the question. "Not recently. But I wish once had been enough for me too."

"Mom!" Hayley hollers from the other end of the ice. "Classes? Remember? Stop flirting and get out here!"

I'm tempted to flip off my own daughter, but this wouldn't go over well in Drayton Corners. Instead, I extend an arm up and David takes my hand to pull me to my feet. His touch lingers a couple beats too long. After an awkward moment, I extract my hand from his.

"Got to run," I say. "I'll see you at the rec center at noon?"

He nods.

I skate off and gather up my seven girls around me, all of whom have their eyes on David as he leaves the building. They don't quite recognize him without his makeup and sunglasses, but there's a hint of curiosity in their eyes.

"We're doing our Ina Bauers again today, girls."

Groans erupt from several. We've been doing this element for weeks. It's a basic skill all figure skaters must master. I quickly demonstrate an inside move and gesture for the girls to show me what they've got, but they freeze, staring at something behind me. I glance back over my shoulder to see a man skating toward us in black, Gore-Tex pants and a red hoodie with the USA logo splashed across the chest. Zeke.

"Hi," he says. "I thought I could help."

I'm momentarily annoyed at the interruption, but it passes when the girls all at once recognize Zeke Smith and begin to titter with excitement.

Swell. A troop of wide-eyed Zeke groupies. "Thank you, David," I reply. "Since you're here, maybe you can demonstrate an inner Ina for the girls?"

He does. Flawlessly. The show-off.

Afterward, I have the girls give it a go, sadly noting they're trying so much harder to get it right for David than they ever do for me. David and I critique and help each one, but he's far more forgiving and praising than I am.

"Now, let's show them how it's really done," David tells me toward the end of class. He holds out his hand. I hesitate, but the kids all stare expectantly at me, so haltingly I grasp his hand, surprised at the spark his touch ignites. His grip is firm and tight, just the way I remember.

With a reluctant surrender, I let him pull me down the ice and we quickly pick up speed. Our outstretched hands together, we glide forward, mirroring each other's stance. With his arm around my waist, we both bend forward on our front leg and stretch out our trailing leg so we slice ahead on one skate in a slow semi-circle. At the end, when both of our skates are back on the ice, he gives me a gentle toss into the air and I let my body spin just once in a simple pirouette, sliding forward on one skate when I land. This move was a basic element of our routine for years and my body remembers it as if we performed it yesterday. At this point in our routine, David would pull me against his chest, but we exchange awkward glances and he releases me. My girls explode in applause. A smile from a lost place inside me breaks out at the memories of skating with him. It's been so long.

David's presence makes a total hash of our morning lessons. The word is out that Zeke Smith is helping Hayley and her mother with lessons, and soon the stands are mobbed with parents. Our students crowd the ice, with those from prior lessons hanging around, refusing to leave. Hayley threw in the towel trying to teach separate lessons, so we combine our last classes of the morning. Twenty-one girls ranging in age from nine to fourteen practice with Hayley, David, and me. Everyone gets a chance to skate with David, while I can't help grinning at my students' excitement and exertion.

"Can you show us some stuff?" one girl, Cami Marsh, asks. The others clap and echo some version of "please."

David chuckles and offers his hand to me. I take it and we skate backward for half a turn around the rink, gathering speed before we flip around, hands together, and race toward the corner. I know exactly what we're doing. He releases my hand and I spin into a simple salchow before gliding backward on one skate. David takes my hand again and pulls me down the ice once more.

I started skating with David when I was ten, and I spent the next seven years with my hand in his almost from the time I awoke until I went to sleep at night. I know what's next, and

I let him toss me into a simple lutz. Then both of us join hands again and race to the other end of the ice. We break apart and launch ourselves into double axels and stick the landings. The applause is musical. No one has cheered an appearance of mine on the ice since I can remember, but then again, they're not really cheering me—it's all about Zeke.

After we're done, David signs ten thousand autographs, poses for a million pictures, and generally chats up a horde of mothers, daughters, and the press. No one approaches me. It's fine. I'm a nobody, and, frankly, I like it this way. I leave David to his adoring fandom and retreat to the locker room to change for the city hall ceremony.

"David Smith," Hayley says, as we strip out of our clothes before showering. "He was your skating partner, Mom. I didn't make the connection at first."

I step beneath the warm shower spray and ignore her. Hayley is showering next to me, and she stares at me expectantly.

"Well?" she presses.

"Yes, David was my skating partner."

"He's the one you won junior gold with?"

"Yes."

We dress in silence. The official town hall ceremony starts in thirty minutes.

"You never told me about him. Why?"

"Can we just drop it? It's a painful subject."

She shakes her head. "No, we can't."

"Fine. What do you want to know?"

"What happened, Mom?"

"Come on, it's time to leave. I'll explain on the way."

On the way from our rink to the new rec center, I glance over at my daughter's expectant face and sigh.

"After David and I won juniors," I begin, "we were the talk of the skating world for months. We wanted to compete at Nationals the next year, so we knew we had to push the envelope with our program."

"And?"

"I wanted more difficult jumps. I wanted to incorporate a throw triple lutz, but David resisted. He didn't think we were ready. Most of the better pairs were doing them and I thought we should step up to the plate. We did well with it in practice, but David wasn't sure we could land it in competition, so we stayed with our standard routine. I was angry. Anyway, in our next event, we did one of our normal throws, but it was all wrong—his toss was off, I landed off, everything was off."

"So you fell," Hayley says with a shrug. "It happens all the time."

"I didn't just fall. I blew out my knee."

Her eyes widen in confusion. "You said you quit." There's a sharp, accusatory tone to her voice.

"I did quit. The doctor said it would take six to nine months for me to recover completely. We all agreed David should temporarily take on a new partner until I was a hundred percent."

"Becky Tisdale," Hayley whispers.

I nod. "You know most of the rest. David started going by Zeke, and he and Becky won at Nationals. They were well on their way to the Olympics for the first time when I was finally able to even attempt skating again. After they won the bronze a month later, temporary became permanent. Of course, four years later they came back and took the gold, and Zeke Smith the movie star was born."

"Oh Mom, I'm sorry."

"Don't be. I'm not." Well, I'm not anymore. "We stayed in touch at first, but during the Olympics broadcast, one of the announcers said me getting injured was the best thing that ever happened to David. That hurt . . . so I stopped calling him. And he stopped calling me. Until yesterday, I hadn't spoken to him since Hanson rocked the radio."

"Who?"

"Never mind. So, now you know everything."

Hayley scowls at me. "Oh, come on, Mom. You two were obviously involved. Admit it. He couldn't take his eyes off of you in there."

I pause, sigh, and nod reluctantly.

"And he broke your heart," she adds.

"I was very young and very naïve."

"So, why didn't you keep skating? Find a new partner?"

"I don't know. I think I was afraid—afraid of failing, afraid of not measuring up to David and Becky. Stupid, huh?"

Hayley gives me a measured look before replying. "No. I get it, Mom."

When we arrive at the rec center, a small crowd has gathered around the front entrance waiting expectantly for the show, such as it is, to begin. Once David arrives in his fancy SUV, we make our way together up to the makeshift dais with a podium and a microphone. At my insistence, Hayley accompanies me. My welcome speech is short, calling Zeke Smith an inspiration and a point of pride for Drayton Corners.

Zeke taps the mike, as if testing whether it's working. "Thanks, Finley. I'm pleased and honored to be here today. I don't know if anyone remembers, but Finley was my first skating partner."

He pauses to glance over at me and smile. I feel a slight flutter in my belly at this. I'm pretty sure no one here remembers David and me and how close we were.

"She embodies the essence of Drayton Corners," he continues. "From her, I learned never to be afraid to try, never to be scared of falling, and never to stay down when you do. It's what Finely is all about, and it's what Drayton Corners is all about. It's what makes this town special. Without those values, I never could have achieved half of what I did. So, thank you, all of you." David leans back from the mike as a burst of applause erupts. I'm blushing redder than an overripe tomato while staring vacantly at my shoes. Then he adds, "Also, if you don't already know, I will be doing a free skating demonstration at the Richter Ice Rink this afternoon at three o'clock. Please join us."

Once the applause ends, I heft a giant pair of silver scissors and hand them to David, unable to avoid his touch. He deftly cuts the white ribbon stretching across the stage in front of us, triggering another round of applause. As the ceremony breaks up, I gesture him over to a bright red, vintage Chevy convertible with a bench seat in back.

"Okay," I say, once we reach the car, "you're supposed to sit on top of the back seat, so everyone can see you."

He balks, and I raise my hands up, palms outward, and nod. "I know. It sounds crazy but talk to Tony. This is his western."

David chuckles softly. "Well, if I have to sit there, you have to sit next me. I'm going to need someone to grab me in case I fall over backward."

"No way. You're the rock star, I'm the local yokel. There are camera crews out there. Tony would have a coronary if he saw my distracting face clogging up the shots."

"Please. Believe me, Tony loves it when I sit next to a beautiful girl. It makes me look desirable."

I playfully slap his shoulder.

Even going five miles an hour, the ride down Main Street only takes about fifteen minutes, although I'm surprised how many people turned out for the parade. Usually only a couple hundred locals watch, but today the sidewalks are jammed with out-of-towners here to see Zeke Smith. I sit next to him and we both wave until my shoulder is ready to fall out of its socket.

Out of the blue, David turns to me and says, "You look amazing, Finny Dean."

His use of my old nickname combined with him slipping his arm around my waist causes my stomach to flip-flop. He called me by this stupid moniker as a rough allusion to Jimmy Dean sausages. It was never flattering, and I can't count the number of times during practices when I'd try to trip him up in retaliation. His hand on my hip feels a little too intimate, but I remind myself this is a media event. We're actors on a stage playing out our assigned parts. So I put my arm around him too, just like I used to do after practice as we skated off the ice to our respective locker rooms. It feels like it all happened yesterday.

"I wanted to cancel this event, you know," he whispers in my ear. "I didn't want to come here, but I had no idea you'd—"

"Still be stuck here?"

"No, that you'd still be here skating. It's like going back in time."

David's skating demonstration at our rink later in the afternoon must be good, because the applause is mostly nonstop. I don't watch, though. Instead, Hayley and I help Gus behind the concession stand. Since we can't charge admission, we're pulling out all the stops to sell concessions.

When David's demonstration ends, the crowd begins to file out, and Hayley and I help Gus close up shop, cleaning dishes and putting away unused food. After a couple hours, I glance down at my watch—five thirty. Good. David is at the airport. I purposely avoided him after the demonstration. He stirred up too many emotions I thought I had left in the past.

"I'll see you later," I tell Hayley. "Take the Toyota. I'll walk home."

Hayley nods in understanding. I do this sometimes. When the rink is dark and the ice is empty, I love to skate alone with my earbuds and iPhone, listening to Brahms. It relaxes me and enables forgetting, and boy do I need to forget today. I slammed the door on my past a long time ago, and I won't let it crack open now. I need to get a grip and stop mooning over what was never meant to be.

The music washes over me like a warm blanket, and I click up the volume. Other than an occasional toe loop, I'm not doing any jumps—simply gliding through parts of our old dance routines. I'm wrapped up in the movement and music so I don't notice at first when a figure skates toward me from the far side of the rink. It's David. He stops ten yards away.

"I thought you had a seven o'clock flight?"

David shrugs. "I rescheduled. Let's skate."

I glance around the rink, expecting to see cameras or a crowd, but we're the only ones in the building.

"David, you don't have to do this anymore. The audience is gone."

He frowns and that may be hurt in his eyes. "You think it's an act, Fin?"

"Yeah. I do."

He skates over to me, takes one of my hands in his, and with his other he gently pulls out my earbuds. Then he lowers his mouth beside my ear, so close his breath tickles the side of my neck.

"Skate with me," he whispers.

Totally flustered, I relent. We skate together for what feels like forever, my hands warmly wrapped in his as he leads me through some of the basic parts of our old program. At one point, we skate backward in each other's arms and ice dance the way we once did. It feels strange and electric to be held in someone's arms again, but this is an illusion. In figure skating, what you see on the ice is carefully choreographed for maximum viewing effect, but it's no more real than the flock snow on your Christmas tree. We break apart and he pulls me along to gain speed, before flipping around backward. David places his hands on my waist and lifts me into the air, while I let my legs scissor open.

"I can't do this," I announce, when he lowers me.

"Okay."

Once we're off the ice, I collapse to the floor and begin reaching for my toes to stretch the muscles in the back of my thighs, ignoring the confused emotions swirling inside me, trying to ignore him. David kneels behind me and begins to massage my shoulders, something he always used to do after practice. I should twist away, but his touch is firm and inviting.

"We're still good together, Fin."

"I better be good. I'm on the ice all day, you know." It's what I have instead of a life. The caress of his hands on my bare shoulders is too distracting so my words peter out.

"I thought a lot about you over the years . . . wondering where you were, how you ended up."

His voice has a wistful tone, which riles me a little, so I cut to the chase. "You said you'd come back for me."

He pauses his massage and he lowers his forehead against the back of my head. "I know. And it's like you're still here waiting for me."

"Finny Dean left the building a long time ago."

"Did she?" When I don't answer, he goes on. "I tried to come back, you know. Many times. But I kept getting sidetracked."

We break apart and I stand.

"You don't owe me an explanation. I don't need pity."

He steps toward me, his face centimeters from mine. "I'm not offering you pity."

Then he gently places his hands on my waist and tugs me into him. I can't do this. He isn't David. He's a stranger who happens to be wearing David's face, but my David never came home. His hands move up to the small of my back.

"Don't," I say. But since I make no move to push him away and my voice is trembling, my command is hollow and empty.

"I'd like to see you again, Fin. I still—"

"No!" I cut him off. "We're from two totally different worlds. You're Zeke. I'm Finley—the girl who runs an antique ice rink in a town with one grocery store."

"Yeah, it won't be easy, but you never wanted easy."

He brushes a stray, sweaty lock of my hair out of my face and I gaze into his blue eyes, almost flinching at their intensity.

"Go back to LA, David. Forget about Drayton Corners and don't come back."

He shakes his head. "Not making that mistake again. Just tell me this—did you feel anything out there on the ice just now? Because I did."

I can't make myself vocalize an answer, so I bite my lower lip and give him the briefest of nods.

"I can't do this," I whisper.

"That's what I said about the triple lutz, remember?"

"You were right."

He shakes his head with a sad expression. "I was wrong. We gave up too fast—I gave up too fast. This time, we stay with it until we stick the landing."

I start to protest more, but I swallow the words when he lowers his lips to mine. Why am I letting this happen to me? The kiss deepens and my defenses melt at its urgency. My fingers find his hair and intertwine themselves in his blond locks. Then I hear the noise of a throat clearing off to our right. Our lips slowly break apart, but I remain in his arms.

"Oops. I'm sorry," Hayley blurts out, acting as if she hasn't been standing there watching us the last five minutes. She gestures with her thumb that she'll wait for me outside and gives me a sly wink.

"Yes," David says, once Hayley is gone.

"Yes what?"

"I'd love to come over for dinner tonight."

"Then kiss me again."

THE END

Love at First Sight
Elizabeth G. Walzel

THE SUN SHONE HIGH and scorching in the South Texas sky when Landon Wells decided to run the fence line of his sprawling ranch, looking for weak links that might be in need of repair. This chore was a pleasure for him, because it gave him the opportunity to enjoy the fresh air and ride his favorite horse, Midnight. Although he allowed his mind to wander a bit, he always kept his eyes sharply focused on the task at hand to ensure that his land and cattle were protected.

During this particular ride along Highway 44, he came across a white Shelby GT350 Mustang that was stopped on the side of the road heading toward Laredo. The smart-looking car seemed abandoned, parked on the shoulder with no one in sight. Knowing how dangerous it was to leave anything along this desolate highway, Landon decided to cross the road to investigate. He tied Midnight to the fence and cautiously approached the vehicle from the rear. Observing that the back seat was empty except for a denim jacket that was draped across the middle and a small, black, quilted overnight bag on the floorboard, he felt a bit more comfortable in continuing his investigation.

Landon began to relax. Rising to his full height of six foot three, he made his way to the front seat, bent at the waist, and looked inside. To his surprise, he saw a petite woman with golden blond hair that was plastered to her forehead with sweat. She was laying slumped in the driver's seat with her head unconsciously resting on her right shoulder. She was beautiful, and even though she was flushed and drenched, Landon felt a rush of emotion drive through his body.

Alarmed now, Landon took his cell phone from his pocket and called his ranch foreman.

"Rey! I'm sending you my coordinates from Highway 44 West toward Laredo. I need you to come right away. This is an emergency, I repeat, emergency. Bring the Suburban, water, and blankets! We have a possible heatstroke victim that needs immediate attention. Hurry! I don't know how long she's been here, but she doesn't look good."

Fueled by adrenaline, Landon began to bang on the window and yell in an attempt to jostle her into consciousness. She only rocked slightly with the force of his body against the car. Deciding that the situation may be dire, he ran back to his horse to grab a shovel and the bottle of water from his saddle pack that he never left home without. Wondering just how long she had been stranded on the side of the highway, he ran to the backseat passenger door and slammed the shovel against the window. It broke and Landon reached in to unlock the door.

"Hey! Hey! Come on now, you need to wake up. Can you hear me?" He patted the side of her cheek, one, two, three times with no semblance of movement. Reaching across her slight, drenched frame, Landon unlocked her car door. Her cheeks were flushed and she was feverish.

"It's okay darlin', I'm just going to come around to your side of the door and get you out of this car. Everything is going to be fine."

Landon raced around to the driver's side of the small vehicle and opened the door. "I gotcha," he softly said as he bent down and gently placed one strong arm under her knees and the other around her narrow shoulders to cradle her neck.

"Here we go. Help is here now. I promise."

He wasn't sure exactly what he was promising, but if she could hear him, he wanted her to feel secure, even though his voice sounded much calmer than he actually felt. His heart pounded loudly in his chest with the fear that was surging through his veins. He couldn't explain why, but somehow he felt responsible for this tiny, blond beauty, who weighed little to nothing in his arms. He felt a possessiveness that told him he just had to make this and anything that got in her way right for her. He needed to help her and keep her safe.

Hearing a fast-approaching vehicle, he knew it was Rey coming to help. He looked up and saw the dust trail floating into the sky behind the racing tires.

"Thank God," he said on an exhale of breath, easily boosting the woman up a little higher across his chest.

Landon looked both ways to make sure his path would be clear crossing the road back onto the right-of-way of his ranch to meet the suburban coming to their rescue. Drawing to an abrupt stop, he could hear Rey throw the truck into park, leaving it running with the air conditioner cooling the interior. Rey opened his door and ran around to the back to open the large vehicle. Gently, Landon placed her onto the makeshift bed Rey had thrown down before leaving the ranch house. Crawling in next to the sleeping woman, he spoke soft soothing words begging her to wake up, and began wetting her lips with the bottled water that he had on hand. Dampening his handkerchief, he gently wiped her forehead in an attempt to lower her blazing hot temperature.

Besides being unconscious, the woman showed signs of fever, profuse sweating, and probably dehydration. He was hoping that she had simply fainted, and hadn't suffered a more serious injury. Excessive thirst and nausea might follow her current symptoms, and if they did, then most likely she was suffering from heat exhaustion rather than heatstroke, which was a much more serious medical emergency.

When they arrived back at the ranch house, Landon placed his hand to her forehead and was glad to note that he had been able to somewhat lower her body temperature. He debated on whether to call for an emergency flight to transfer her quickly to the nearest hospital, when she began to stir. His relief was palpable, although they were not in the clear yet. Rocking her head back and forth as if she was dreaming, she began to utter nonsensical words, and so he continued to stroke her forehead and whisper soothing words of encouragement.

***

"That's right. You can do it. Come on lil' darlin', wake up." He wiped her face with his dampened kerchief, continuing to speak softly to this unexpected guest.

She began to mumble on her journey back to consciousness. "Wha—? What happened?" Her eyes fluttered, as she tried to bring them into focus.

When she looked up into Landon's Caribbean blue eyes, she seemed bewildered and mesmerized at the same time. Several moments passed before either one spoke.

"What happened? Where am I?" Her voice was small.

"Thank God." Landon looked up in praise. "You had us worried. You're safe here and it looks like you are going to be alright," Landon said as if he had been holding his breath. He removed his hand from her forehead and placed it over her hand, which was resting on her stomach. He smiled reassuringly. "I found you passed out in your car back on Highway 44, and brought you here to my ranch. Can you remember anything?"

"I'm not sure. It kind of feels fuzzy, like a dream, but I remember that I was headed to Laredo. I think my car was beginning to overheat. That's when I decided to pull onto the shoulder." Her voice was little more than a whisper. Landon raised her head and offered her a sip of water, then gently laid her head back on the pillow where it had been resting.

"I was only going to turn it off long enough for it to cool and I must have dozed off before realizing how hot I was getting. The next thing I knew, I was waking up here with you." Her full lips began to quiver as if she were going to cry, and Landon smiled at her reassuringly.

"Well, now don't you worry about a thing. You are welcome to stay here as long as you need to until you feel strong enough to continue your trip. I usually take my horse, Midnight, out in the morning. I'm just glad we waited until the afternoon today or we may not have found you. You gave us quite a fright, but I think we are dealing with heat exhaustion, rather than heatstroke, which is good.

My name is Landon King, and this is my ranch."

"Livy. My name is Livy Wagner." Her throat was still parched from the dehydration and she coughed a little trying to clear her voice.

"Here, take another sip of water."

Her eyes, which had been locked on his, shifted to their hands comfortably resting together, hers inside of his. When Landon's eyes followed her line of sight, he abruptly pulled his hand away, having forgotten that he was holding hers. He missed her warmth the second he moved. He couldn't explain his instinctive need to protect this woman, or the instant attraction he felt when he looked at her.

Livy felt something too. Maybe it was because this man had saved her. After all, her thoughts were a bit scrambled from the heat exhaustion she had experienced. What did she know about this man really? Not one thing; well, with the exception that he had done a very good deed for her. But, for some reason, when he moved his hand from hers, she missed the comfort of his touch, feeling as though she might have just lost something special. She did not understand why this stranger could have such an effect on her, but she was interested in finding out.

He was tall and lean with broad shoulders and a narrow waist. His eyes were like pools of blue water and she felt that if she let herself, she could get lost in them. His skin was tanned and slightly weathered from the harsh Texas elements. His hair was dark and a little long, but in a good way, with curls that whispered around his ears and collar. His legs seemed to go on forever, and he knew how to wear a pair of jeans. He wore western boots made of ostrich, and a crisp white shirt. His hat was straw and the combination of all of these things added up to a drool-worthy package. Her heartbeat sped up as she took him in.

"Livy, hmmm?" His voice was deep in appreciation. "Well now, that's a real pretty name for a very pretty little lady," he said with a boyish grin. "How are you feeling? Is there anything I can get you? We need to be careful to monitor your liquids for a while until we are sure that you are feeling back to normal."

"I'm beginning to feel better, thank you." Livy blushed, which Landon found endearing.

"So, what were you doing driving toward Laredo all by yourself?" Landon asked.

Livy hesitated before answering but decided to be honest with her rescuer. "My daddy is Cinco Wagner. You may have heard of him. We have the W Ranch near Goliad."

"No kidding." Landon smiled with recognition. "Yes, I actually met your father at an auction a few years ago. I bought some of his cattle for my ranch. He has a very good reputation."

She smiled at this. "That's him. He is an amazing man and a loving father."

Landon looked at her. "I don't mean to typecast, but you don't look as though you would have much ranching experience."

"Well then," she said, "it will surprise you to know that I've been riding horseback since I could walk. But you're actually right, that's pretty much all I know about living on a ranch. I grew up in Austin with my Mama and was sent to boarding schools from the time I was twelve. My Mama's sweet as pie, but she is as strong-willed as a bull."

Landon loved the southern lilt in her soft voice and laughed in response to her comparison.

"She didn't want me growing up on the ranch because she thought I would become a wild tomboy," Livy went on. She laughed a little at the thought, looking down at her small delicate hands, remembering her parents discussing it. "Mama got her way, just as she always did with Daddy, and as you can see," her arms spread across her body, "I am anything *but* a tomboy. I grew up in luxury and lace, not cowboy boots and a hat, although I would have loved growing up on the ranch. I spent every vacation possible there.

"That still doesn't tell me why you were heading toward Laredo all by yourself."

"Well, it's complicated. You see, I turned 24 a few weeks ago. I have a master's degree in ranch management, which Mama was totally against, but it made Daddy happy. Anyway, I decided that I wanted to go and stay with Daddy at the ranch for a bit. You know, to try to get some practical experience and put my degree to good use. Most importantly though, I wanted to spend time with Daddy."

"Okay . . . " Landon prompted her, interested in every word she was saying, but at the same time wanting her to get to the point.

"By the way . . . is my car still out on the highway?" The musical sound of her voice went up in pitch with her question.

Landon smothered a laugh at her unexpected change in subject. "No, your keys were in the car, so I had Rey drive it to the ranch for safekeeping. I had to break a window to get to you, so that needs to be replaced, and we need to find the trouble that caused it to overheat. Fixing your vehicle might take a few days."

"Oh my goodness. Well, thank you. I hope it's not too much trouble."

"I have a full-time mechanic on the ranch, so it's no trouble whatsoever. Now, will you please get back to your explanation?"

"Yes. Well, Daddy had an 'episode'." She made quotation marks with her fingers. "He wouldn't call it what it was, which was a mild heart attack, about a week before I was able to get to him." She looked back up into Landon's eyes. "His doctor said that he needed to take it easy, which if you know my Daddy, you know that is a very tall order."

Landon smiled at her assessment.

"When I got to the W, Daddy looked tired, you know?" She paused as she recalled. "He had lost quite a bit of weight since Christmas, and he seemed a little . . . well, depressed." She looked up into those deep blue eyes. "At that moment, I knew it was going to be up to me to take care of him and make sure he made a full recovery."

"Laredo?" Landon sounded a bit exasperated, even though he really wasn't.

"Oh, yes, well as I mentioned before, I have my master's in ranch management," she smirked at him teasingly, "so I'm headed down to Laredo to meet with our accountant and attorneys. I hope to examine the business records of the ranch so that I can be useful during my stay." She was flirting with him now, finally offering him the explanation he wanted.

Landon let out a breath that he didn't realize he was holding. Laughing, he said, "Finally!" They both laughed at their inside joke.

"Oh, that reminds me, is there someone at home that you should call to let them know your whereabouts?"

"No, not tonight. I hate to admit it, but I am tired. I'll call to check in tomorrow, if you are sure that I won't be too much of an inconvenience to you."

"Don't you worry about that," he said smiling. "We have plenty of room here. Do you feel like you can walk?"

"I think so," she said as she attempted to do just that. Upon rising, her head began to swim, causing her to sway, slightly losing her balance. Landon steadied her by putting his arm around her tiny waist and helped her to the guest room.

"This is your room, just off of the living area. That way you can call out if you need anything during the night. I think you will be comfortable here. It was my little sister's room when she lived here."

When Livy entered the room, she felt right at home. It was lovely and spacious, hosting a king-size bed with a canopy that was decorated in gorgeous bedding. Soft pillows rested at the head of the bed, which was already pulled down for her to snuggle into. There was even a chocolate mint on her pillow. She smiled at the sight, turned to Landon and thanked him for his generosity. She grinned as he reddened at the praise.

"Your overnight bag is on the dresser. The bathroom is through that door," he nodded his head to the corner of the room, "and there are towels and toiletries set out for your use."

"A bath would be great. To tell the truth, I feel a little spent. Do you know what time it is?"

"It's 4:45 p.m. You have time for a nice nap before supper which is usually served around seven. Does that sound good?"

"It sounds perfect."

***

Mrs. Harper had been cooking for the Kings since Landon was a baby. She loved him like a grandson and treated him like one too. She spoiled him and kept him in line depending on what was called for at the time, and their relationship hadn't changed much in the thirty years she had been around.

She was the best cook in the county and Landon told her so most every day of his life. This night was no exception; she had prepared a meal that was comforting and nutritious, a talent that Landon often wished he could bottle to sell, telling her they would make a fortune. He knew he had it good with Mrs. Harper—after all, she had been a constant in his life, and he cherished her for it.

When Landon and Livy entered the dining room the table had been set for two and a small bouquet of flowers were placed in the center of the table in a small vase.

"Mrs. Harper, this is Livy Wagner. She will be staying with us for a few days."

"Hello Livy, it is so nice to meet you. Landon told me all about your dreadful afternoon. How are you feeling, dear?" Her green eyes were kind and her smile genuine as she extended her hand.

"I'm feeling much better Mrs. Harper. Thank you so much for your kind hospitality. Dinner smells so wonderful. I can't remember if I ate lunch or not, but I certainly am hungry."

"Mrs. Harper," Landon said, "shouldn't we set another place at the table?"

Mrs. Harper lived onsite in a guest house that Landon's parents built just for her, and she usually shared her meals with the family.

"No, darling, not tonight. Remember, I have my bridge game at Claire's house."

Landon nodded, "Of course. Well, have fun. And as always, thank you for an amazing meal. Be careful, and don't forget to call if you need anything."

Mrs. Harper excused herself and left through the kitchen door. Landon pulled out a chair for Livy and motioned for her to take her seat.

"Landon, I want to thank you again for saving me this afternoon, and for allowing me to stay here until my car is fixed."

"Nonsense. It's really no trouble." He lifted the platter of pot roast and set it in front of Livy's plate for her to serve herself. Once she did, he continued offering her plates that included fresh corn on the cob, mashed potatoes, and green beans. They made easy conversation while enjoying their meal, and their connection seemed to strengthen as they got to know each other.

"Livy?"

She looked up from her plate and into his deep blues. There was concern in them and she responded with a questioning glance.

"Hmm?"

"I'm planning to go to Laredo day after tomorrow for supplies. I was wondering if you would like to go with me? We could grab some lunch and then go to your appointments. I always pick up my supplies on my way back out of town."

"I think that would be nice, Landon. I'll look forward to it."

When they finished dinner, they cleared the table, setting the dishes in the sink as Mrs. Harper had insisted. Landon placed his hand on the small of Livy's back to lead her into the living room.

"Would you like a brandy or some other kind of nightcap?"

"That sounds delightful."

Livy settled on the sofa as Landon poured the dark liquid into decorative brandy snifters. Making his way back to her, he handed her the tiny glass and she felt his fingers brush against hers, sending a shiver right to her core.

Landon's attraction to her grew more intense at their touch. But his instinct to protect her was enough to keep his roaming thoughts in check. She had experienced a very difficult day and was in no condition to face the onslaught of emotions that had raced through his mind ever since he had lifted her small frame out of the car. No, he would wait. After all, he'd never been a "player" so to speak, even though he had definitely been around. He was considered quite the catch among the ladies and was used to getting their attention without ever having to actually work for it. But Livy was different and it confused him.   He didn't believe in love at first sight, that would be absurd, but if he did, he would have to admit that Cupid was having a bit too much fun with him. This beautiful woman had, somehow, gotten under his skin. And he wanted to know her in every way.

Livy was captivated by the intensity of his gaze. Her heart began to pound in her ears, and she couldn't help but worry that the heat building inside of her would rise up and reveal itself with a blush. *Could he possibly be feeling the same as I do?* The mere thought caused her breathing to quicken. Looking down at her last sip of brandy, she tipped the glass into her mouth. A final drip escaped and rested invitingly on her full lower lip which she seductively caught with a slow lick.

"I'd better turn in for the night," Livy said softly.

"I think that's a good idea. Goodnight, Livy. If you need anything during the night or get confused about where you are, just holler. I will be upstairs in my room, but I'll leave the door open."

She smiled. "Goodnight."

***

Livy awoke the next morning and stretched contentedly in the glow of a good night's sleep. Going through her overnight bag, she found a pair of distressed skinny jeans and a V-neck t-shirt and got dressed. Grateful to have packed her one pair of western boots, she added them to her outfit, pulled her shoulder length blond hair back into a ponytail and made her way to breakfast.

"Mrs. Harper! Good morning."

"Well, good morning to you too dear. How are you feeling?"

"Oh, much better, thank you. How was your bridge game?"

Smiling, Mrs. Harper replied, "We actually talk more than play, but it's always fun to get out and see friends. Are you hungry?"

"No thank you. It's already so late. I usually don't sleep in, but I must have needed it after yesterday. I'll wait for lunch if that's okay." Looking around the room, Livy continued, "Do you know where Landon is this morning?" She tried not to sound overly interested.

"He is out on Midnight riding the fence lines again. He's generally up, fed, and out the door between five thirty and six every morning, and the first thing he does is take Midnight out for a ride before beginning his chores around the ranch. I think it was fate that he went out in the afternoon yesterday and found you."

Livy looked at the older woman, considering her words. She tried to mask her disappointment of missing a chance to see Landon this morning.

"Oh, I almost forgot dear, he left a note for you." Mrs. Harper pulled a folded piece of paper from her apron and handed it to her.

"He did? Thank you." At this news, Livy's spirits lifted. She opened the note slowly, as though it were breakable and began to silently read.

Good morning, Livy.

I trust you had a restful night and hope you are feeling better today. I will be in to have lunch around noon and would like you to join me if you are up to it. Please take it easy and make yourself at home.

Until then,

Landon

Livy couldn't hide her smile, and the excitement that coursed through her veins at knowing she would see him again in just two hours. When she looked up, Mrs. Harper gave her an understanding smile.

***

Lunch was delicious, and the company was too. Landon walked in a few minutes before noon, just as he said he would, and headed straight to the washroom to freshen up after being outside all morning. When he reentered the living room, where Livy waited, his smile broadened, and the sight melted Livy. He made his way over to her in three long strides, and without hesitation, he wrapped his arms around her, giving her a warm hug. Her feet practically left the floor and she giggled. He smelled like man: all outdoorsy, like hay, sunshine, and soap. Livy took it all in and let him envelop her in his strong embrace. She could fall for this man, she thought, and maybe already had. Feeling embarrassed by her reaction, she pulled back slightly to peer into his eyes. His hold on her loosened a bit, but he didn't put her down.

Landon's voice was husky as he looked down into her beautiful olive-colored eyes. "I missed you this morning."

"You did?" Livy responded somewhat breathlessly.

"Mmhmm." His head nodded in a yes motion. "I did." He leaned in and whispered in her ear. "I couldn't help but think of you sleeping downstairs, all by yourself, with me upstairs, all by myself."

Livy shivered at his words. "Well, aren't you a sweet talker?"

"I'm just telling you how it is for me, Liv. I don't know what it is about you that has turned my heart inside out, but I am willing to take whatever time is necessary to find out." Landon smiled and placed a kiss on her forehead.

"Well, I suppose, since we are being honest with each other," she said shyly, "I should admit that you seem to have had the same effect on me, Landon." She looked back up to see his reaction and her breath left her.

He looked deeply into her eyes, his mouth close to hers, and then he gently pressed his lips to hers. She felt his heat drive right through her, and when he licked the crease of her closed mouth, she opened for him, inviting him in. That was all the invitation he needed. Landon tightened his hold around her small frame as he pressed into her mouth, probing and exploring, and she responded as though they were absolutely meant to be there, together, like this, until the day when there could be more.

A bell rang from the dining room, breaking the spell that they had seemed to cast around each other. Livy could feel them both smile, lip to lip, knowing that this was the sign from Mrs. Harper that lunch was being served. Reluctantly, they pulled away from each other, both looking a little grief-stricken at the loss of the intimacy they'd shared.

"You hungry?" Landon asked, and all Livy could do was nod her head yes.

***

The day in Laredo was more play than work. While Landon and Livy managed to accomplish the tasks they'd planned, the majority of the day was spent enjoying each other and having fun. They were growing very close even though they had known each other less than a week.

Livy called home, as she said she would, with Landon sitting right beside her. She let her family know where she was, and that she was alright. Her daddy remembered Landon as a well-liked and well-respected young man.

"Baby doll, hand the phone over to Landon so I can thank him properly for rescuing my little girl."

"Mr. Wagner?" Landon said.

"Landon, I just want to thank you personally for saving my baby girl. She means the absolute world to me and the very thought of her being broken down on the side of that highway all alone is just more than this old heart can take. Son, I owe ya."

Grinning, Landon responded, "Mr. Wagner, believe me when I say, it has been my pleasure getting to know Livy. You know, she may have actually been the one who saved me. She's a very special woman, and I intend to spend a lot more time with her now and in the future."

"Son, I said I owe ya, but . . . " he joked.

Landon laughed. "Yes sir, I'm going to hold you to it."

Their conversation ended in laughter, with an invitation to the W Ranch for a barbecue to be given in their honor. Of course, Landon agreed and thanked Cinco in advance. They hung up and he enveloped Livy in a big bear hug that quickly heated, as was their new norm.

Landon remembered the day they met and the promise he made to her. At the time, he wasn't sure exactly what he was promising, but he did now. He was promising her forever. And Cupid? Well, Cupid made a believer out of Landon, because he now believed in love at first sight.

THE END

Auld Lang Syne
Gerald Winter

S HE HAD SEEN THE dress in a custom tailor shop on the boulevard the week before. The dress was worn by a mannequin with its arms and legs cut off at the elbows and knees, and displayed in the store's window like Venus de Milo on a pedestal.

"Is it a *shift*?" I asked as we stood outside the dress shop. An old girlfriend had described her prom gown that way in high school. The dress was strapless with translucent lace across the bust, and was hemmed a few inches above the knees. All black, it was simple, but meant to draw attention to the curves and swells of the woman who would shape it.

"It says *chemise* on the sign," she said as we huddled close that cold December evening, already almost dark before five o'clock. Multi-colored lights flashed around the window with the holiday season in full array.

A handwritten note was pinned to the waistline and written in both English and Korean. I understood only the English, but Para understood both. She was neither fluent nor fully literate in her second language after a decade of living in America. However, our intimacy in nose-to-nose conversations for hours over the past year had vastly improved her English outside her sheltered Korean society within America. Since leaving Seoul, she had come here by way of California then had lived in Flushing, New York for a year. After that, she had found a basement apartment in Palisades Park, New Jersey where most store front signs were in both Hangul characters and English. We had been sharing her apartment for almost that entire year.

"There's no price on it," I said, my words emitting vapor in the frigid air.

"The sign in Korean says, 'price negotiable according to tailoring.' I want to go inside," Para said.

I couldn't imagine trying to learn a language that could say so much with so few written strokes. She'd told me that Hangul doesn't express words but rather ideas and emotions. I imagined they were much like Para's facial expressions—subtly concise.

I'd once asked her if she was angry with me for doubting her love. I'd made a jealous gesture over her friendships with other men when we'd first dated. She'd continued those friendships after we'd expressed our love for each other and I'd objected. Her face had revealed no expression at my request that she cut off those men, but her silence had made me think she was angry.

"Are you angry because I'm jealous?" I'd asked.

"I could never be angry with you," she'd said, easing my concern, but only for a moment. "But I am *disappointed*."

In a second, I'd realized I'd prefer her to be angry with me. Disappointing Para because of my behavior felt like a knife through my heart. I'd vowed never to disappoint her again and always to trust her and our love for each other as the purest truth we would ever know.

"Love is not possessing," she had said. "True love is letting go."

"You say that," I'd said in jest, "but wouldn't you be angry and jealous if you learned that I had made love to another woman?"

"If you did it only to hurt me, yes," she'd said. "But if you needed to, I would never object or love you any less. Men are weak when it comes to this. I won't lose you by trying to change the tides of a thousand seas. As I shall endure, so will our love."

I'd felt a hollowness in my heart, telling her, "But you must expect the same from me. I couldn't endure your unfaithfulness. I'd be angry."

"Men are selfish," she'd said with a shrug. "I have no control over how you would feel, but I do over how I would react to how you feel. Consider yourself already forgiven. Our love is forever. Foolish things we may say or do during our journey have nothing to do with our love or who we really are. Not if we won't let them. I won't let foolishness change our true course."

"Me neither," I'd vowed, but wondered if I'd have the strength to keep that promise.

***

Inside the dress shop, Para bargained with the elderly Korean woman about the black dress. She measured Para and jotted some notes in Hangul, then took the dress on the mannequin from the window and marked it with chalk according to her notes. Para smiled broadly at me, her perfect teeth like brilliant pearls. She prided herself for never having had a cavity at age forty. She said she owed it to tofu, brown rice, and kimchi. She hadn't tasted cheese until age thirty when she had arrived in LA where she'd studied nursing and worked at a hospital in Korea Town. She'd followed a boyfriend to the East Coast and had settled in northern Jersey. She hadn't spoken much about her former boyfriend, only occasional references to "Joe."

Occasionally her cell would ring, and she'd say hello in Korean and head to the bathroom in our apartment. When I'd start to say something, she'd put her index finger to her lips and shake her head. Seeing the quandary in my expression, she'd cover her cell and whisper, "It's only Joe." Then she'd close the bathroom door behind her and turn on the fan. All I could hear was her muffled tone in Korean through the door.

When she'd come out of the bathroom twenty minutes later to see my look of frustration, she'd nestle beside me on the sofa and say she was sorry, that it was only Joe, no reason to be upset. Joe had been her friend for twenty years. They'd met in Korea when he had worked there, and he had convinced her to come to America where she would find a better life. She loved America, but her soul would always be Korean.

We'd been together a year when I asked her to marry me. She said she didn't want to be married, that she wanted to be a free spirit, that marriage often spoiled true love. When she saw my pain, she embraced me and told me her family story in Korea when she was known by her birth name—Keum Suk . . .

Yoju, Korea

When Keum Suk heard her father's harsh tone toward her mother, Bong, she covered her ears and curled her knees to her chest as she lay on the thin floor mat she called her bed. For months, Keum watched her mother's decline with her father's lengthy absences and stormy returns. Bong sought comfort in her daughter's arms. Keum embraced her mother as they both shuddered and wept. Alone in the dark, they rocked, and Bong sang to her, caressing Keum's head and wiping away her tears till morning.

Keum's father, Kim Jae Lee, farmed his fertile land in Yoju southeast of Seoul. The eldest son of a middleclass family, Kim had inherited fifty acres when his mother died in 1952. Keum's grandmother was a strong woman, but the hardships of war and the separation from her two sisters in North Korea had aged her quickly.

Though Keum's grandmother did not live to see peace come in 1953, Bong told Keum, "Your father's mother was too attached to her sisters in the north to appreciate her son's hard work here on the farm. Her heart was no longer in this world, but she is at peace in Buddha's Garden, so don't fret for her. If you wish to be happy in your life, you must find peace from within yourself. Joy and love come from within, not from this harsh material world."

As an adolescent, Keum thought long about what her mother had said. She sensed no bitterness in her mother's words, but rather resolution. Keum did not understand the conflict between her parents until a woman ten years younger than her mother came to their farmhouse with a boy at her side, both carrying luggage. Keum watched curiously from the chicken coop where she gathered that morning's eggs. Keum knew this young woman came from the city by her dress and manners—polite but curt. The boy had no manners and grimaced at the rural surroundings with his nose scrunched in offense to the farm's stench of dung.

Keum picked a bouquet of wild flowers, draped them in her egg basket, and brought them to the house as a peace offering for her mother's guest, who gradually revealed her belligerence. Though Bong remained cordial, Keum noticed her mother's hands shook with the high pitch of the intruder's grating tone.

"My son must have his own room," the young woman demanded. "You must share with your daughter. I will share the main bedroom with Kim . . . " She paused as Keum shyly presented the wildflowers to her. The young woman looked down into Keum's wondering eyes and took the flowers. "Your daughter has a good heart. *Kamsamnida.*" She thanked Keum with a brush of her hand under Keum's chin.

Keum liked the unfamiliar floral scent of the woman's hand, so different from her mother's aroma of rice and dumplings and the tang of *kimchi*, offensive to those who didn't eat the spicy pickled cabbage every day.

Bong pulled Keum away from the woman and hugged her close to her bosom. Her bottom lip quivered as she spoke. "I can only hope Kim will tire of you . . . but it is not for me to interfere with his desires. I expect some help inside the house, but I know you are unaccustomed to the labors of a farm. My daughter and I can manage, but your son can be of use. Kim would want him to learn how to farm his land."

"Perhaps you are right, but *Kim* will direct Yung, not I, and certainly not you. He is *our* son, not yours," the younger woman said with disrespect.

"Then bring in your luggage. There is fresh fruit if you like, but Keum and I must finish our duties before dark. My hus—" she caught herself. "Kim will be back from the market in two hours. We'll prepare the rice and kimchi. He will be hungry."

She nodded and directed Yung to bring in their luggage. As Keum passed him to complete her chores in the field, Yung stuck out his foot and tripped her. She fell, scuffing her knees and elbows to protect the basket of eggs in her hands. Only one broke, and Bong whispered that it was all right, but Keum glared at the smirking Yung. When he glared back, she experienced fear for the first time. This young woman and her son toppled Keum's world, but when her mother shuddered beside her in bed that night to the sound of her father's panting and the young woman's shrieks from the next room, Keum's outlook changed forever . . .

***

The old Korean woman at the dress shop told Para that she wanted ninety-five dollars for the black chemise, including the tailoring and accessories, which included a small, lacquered black purse with a thin shoulder strap.

"How much?" I asked Para as we returned a week later to pick up the dress.

As I took a crisp new Franklin from my wallet, Para grasped my forearm. After a lively exchange between the shopkeeper and Para, the old woman nodded with a crooked grin. Para leafed through my wallet with nimble fingers, taking four twenties and handing them to the shopkeeper. We bowed to one another with expressions of thanks in both languages, and I carried the box containing the dress and the purse under one arm as Para clung to the other.

The sidewalk on the boulevard was hazardous with patches of ice from a snowstorm earlier that week. Mounds of snow still lined the street where parking spots had been carved out with shovels. Our breaths blew back in our faces with crystalized vapor that stung our flushed cheeks. As we walked back toward our apartment against the wind, we heard Christmas carols from the shops along the way. We stopped to the chime of a skinny old Korean man dressed as Santa Claus who was slumped beside a cardboard chimney soliciting Salvation Army donations.

I thought I was generous reaching for my last twenty-dollar bill to put into the chimney, but Para's gloved hand grabbed me by the wrist as she nodded to the Franklin I'd intended to give the old woman for Para's black chemise.

With a sigh I dropped the c-note into the chimney, and said to Para, "I thought you'd agreed to pay her ninety-five dollars for the dress."

"She'd be insulted if I didn't bargain for a better price," Para said. "If I'd let you give her that hundred-dollar bill, it would have been an insult to *you*. We settled on seventy-five. The rest was a tip for her kindness and skill. I also told her that you were a bestselling American writer, so she should be flattered that you saw her dress in the window and came into her shop to buy it for me."

"Selling? Maybe. But *best?* Only because you love me. The old woman seemed pleased."

"Of course," Para said with a chortle. "She would have settled for *sixty* dollars."

We laughed, squeezing each other in our overcoats with our scarves wrapped around our necks. She saw from my expression how much I wanted to kiss her, but she squinted one eye to remind me that public demonstrations of affection, even between husbands and wives, was unacceptable in Korean society. For all intents and purposes, Palisades Park was Seoul, Korea. What Para held back from me on the street was more than made up for as we thawed out in our apartment drinking hot green tea with honey.

Our table Christmas tree was lit, and the smell of blue spruce permeated the room as we played Christmas carols on CDs and cuddled beneath the silk sheets in our king-size bed. Our red noses were still cold as we kissed, making us laugh. Hours later we were hungry, and Para prepared a special *doku* soup with shrimp and tofu and dumplings which made our stomachs growl. After the soup we returned to bed with her cheek resting on my chest and her long black hair draped down to my thighs. I felt as if we'd become one person and that life could never be better than that moment.

We dozed off for an hour, then when we woke, Para kneeled on the bed and looked toward the black chemise hanging from the door and her shiny black purse with its thin leather strap over the hook. A pair of designer black heels stood at the base of the door. All that was missing from that image was Para. She cocked her head back and forth as if taking measure of her new dress.

She spoke my thoughts: "I'll wear it tomorrow when you take me to Radio City for the Christmas Show and the Rainbow Room for dinner and dancing till midnight. It will be the best Christmas ever. I'll feel like Cinderella. I'm afraid the black chemise will turn to rags at the stroke of midnight and the best day of our life together will be lost. I don't ever want to lose that day. I want to wear the black chemise forever. I want you to always see me that way . . . promise that's how you'll always see me."

"Of course," I said, pulling her close. "I'll love you forever."

***

We enjoyed the Christmas Show at Radio City and then walked around the skating rink at Rockefeller Plaza to take in the beauty of the enormous Christmas tree with the sounds and scents of Manhattan turning our special day into a winter wonderland to remember forever.

In the Rainbow Room, Para was glad to remove her overcoat, so she could display her black chemise on the dance floor. We ate and danced from eight to eleven that night, then she whispered as we danced cheek-to-cheek, "We have to make it home by midnight—Cinderella."

I started to object, but when she pulled away I saw her earnest expression.

"Hurry," she said later as we turned off the boulevard onto our side street. It was 11:55 p.m.

"We've had a bottle of wine," I said, patting her knee beside me in the car. "I don't want to celebrate Christmas with a DUI. I have to be able to drive you to the doctor tomorrow for your checkup."

"Quick! Into the apartment," she said as I parked. She didn't wait for me to open the car door for her.

"Take it easy," I cautioned her. "Especially in those heels. The sidewalk is icy."

She kicked off her heels and scampered down the steps to the apartment, hopping on the welcome mat to keep her stocking feet from freezing. She shivered as I unlocked the door, then burst into the warm apartment. She'd dropped one high-heeled shoe on the mat behind her, making me laugh as I picked it up and thought *Cinderella.*

She removed her dress and hung it back on the door. She took her cell phone, lipstick, and a package of tissues from the purse and hung it on the hook with the dress. We made love for an hour before she fell asleep in my embrace. Moonlight shone through the bedroom window giving the black chemise a bluish cast where it hung on the back of the bedroom door. I blinked, imagining Para in the dress, so full of life that evening. The image of the dress hanging on the door remained in my mind as I drifted into slumber.

***

The aroma of an omelet cooking stirred my senses the next morning. My mind had kept the memory of the black chemise on the door, but it quickly faded when I saw the empty hook.

"*Choen achime!*" I called good morning to Para where she was busily preparing our breakfast and setting the table. I got out of bed and put on my bathrobe then embraced her from behind at the stove. "Where's the dress?" I asked.

"Turned to rags at the stroke of midnight," she said, bumping me with her hip. Then she turned and saw my frown. "I put it away for *next* Christmas." She laughed like a child. "It will take years, but eventually it will turn to rags. I am Cinderella, I really am."

Later that afternoon, we sat in the waiting room for our appointment to see her doctor. She wouldn't consider seeing an American doctor even though Dr. Kim smoked at his desk as he asked her medical questions in Korean. Then he turned to me to say the same in English.

"There could be a problem," he said.

I turned to Para and saw tears in her eyes.

"I told her about the calcification on her X-ray three months ago, but she's ignored my recommendation. The results of her mammogram from a week ago show what may be Stage 4 cancer in her right breast. She needs to see an oncologist this afternoon. Here's the information for your appointment at three o'clock . . . I'm sorry."

***

Memories of Christmas quickly faded. A mastectomy followed by radiation and chemo took up all of spring and most of the summer. Wearing her wig, Para rode her bicycle beside me in Overpeck Park and showed regaining strength from the ordeal. There were autumn leaves in full color on Korean Thanksgiving. We celebrated in the park with many smoky barbecues stirring our appetites. After that celebration, Para didn't want to sit around the apartment every day worrying about her condition and whether it would continue to metastasize or go into remission.

She took a job as a receptionist for a Korean chiropractor within walking distance of our apartment. Getting out on weekdays for six hours brightened her spirits and gave me time to write without watching her every move to be sure she did everything her oncologist said for her to do. Except when she took off her wig at night or changed clothes and her surgery scars showed where her breast had been, Para seemed perfectly healthy. She hadn't vomited from nausea in weeks and had been eating normally. Color had returned to her often-smiling face.

Before we knew it, December had come again. Though at minimum wage, Para's meager salary was off the books, so she was preparing envelopes with cash as gifts to her Korean friends for Christmas. She marked each envelope with a friend's Korean-adapted English name so I'd know whom each envelope was for.

"This one's for Alice," she'd say. "You know her as *Grumpy Girl.* This one's for Yuji, *Ugly Girl*, and that one's for Stacey, *Boring Girl.*"

I laughed at her serious expression as she told me this, which reminded me of her English Study Manual with a sedate Korean woman on the cover, apparently a well-known actress in Seoul. When I'd helped Para practice her conversational

English, I'd asked her to give me the English expression to excuse herself to use the bathroom.

With her bright smile, Para said, as if she were at a cocktail party at the White House: "Pardon me, but I have to take a dump."

My mouth dropped open. "No way!" I said. "Let me see that."

Sure enough that was the translation in the manual. Every time I saw that Korean actress's face on the cover, I couldn't keep from laughing till my eyes teared. As usual, Para punched my shoulder and said with inflection, "Please excuse me, I want to use the ladies' room."

The pain in my shoulder from her punch gave me confidence that she was surely regaining her strength in remission.

Two weeks before Christmas, Para bought a wind-up Christmas toy of a fluffy stuffed rabbit the size of a teddy bear, with dangling ears. Wound up, the rabbit would play "Auld Lyne Syne" on a saxophone as it gyrated to the melody. Whenever I wound it and played the song, Para would mimic the rabbit's gyrations and we'd both laugh joyously. It became our foreplay to making love for the holidays.

The week before Christmas, Para hung the black chemise on the back of our bedroom door with the purse hanging by its strap and the high-heeled black shoes at the base of the door.

"I want you take me dancing again," she said, nodding to the dress. "This time on New Year's Eve."

"Of course," I said. "Whatever you want."

***

The Monday after Christmas we waited in the oncologist's office for the results of Para's scan taken the week before. Usually spirited and often whistling in past visits, the oncologist seemed glum in his silence. Then his five words hit me like the thuds of nails into a coffin: "It's metastasized into her liver."

When I translated for Para, she said, "But I feel fine."

"I'm sorry," the doctor said, "but it won't be long before you don't."

"What can we do?" I asked with a lump in my throat.

"Enjoy yourselves for as long as you can; when the pain begins there's hospice."

My head jerked back and forth from him to Para as she wept.

"How much time does she have?"

He just shook his head. It was anybody's guess.

I clutched her prescription for pain as we headed to the car, wondering if I kept from filling it, maybe the pain would never come. I put it off until the next day because she hadn't complained of any pain and had only smiled at me with watery eyes. We spent the next day in bed just holding each other and staring at the black chemise hanging on the door. She had no appetite and neither did I.

The day before New Year's Day she stared at me when she woke. Her eyes were glassy, and her pupils were dilated.

"I'll get the prescription filled," I said. "Should I call for hospice?"

She shook her head. "Don't be long," she said with shallow breath.

It took me no longer than twenty minutes to return to our apartment with the pain-killing drug. The drapes were drawn in our bedroom, so it was too dark to see our bed when I first opened the door. As light poured in from the hall, I saw that the black chemise was missing, but the purse and the shoes remained.

"Para," I called softly to her, but got no response. I pulled the drapes open just enough to see her crumpled form on the bed, dressed in the black chemise. My heart sank and I was short of breath as I rushed to lift her, leaning her against my chest. The satin sheets were soiled and dried blood from her nose ran down to her chin.

"Keum Suk!" I shouted. "Para!"

Para was her Christian name, given to her by the nuns when she'd become a Roman Catholic in Seoul at age twenty-seven. She had told me over the past two years much about her life before we had met: her disappointment with her father when he'd brought his mistress and their children into her home, and how her mother had died young of a broken heart. She'd feared her step-brothers when her mother had passed, but her father had given her enough money to leave the farm and get a college education in Seoul.

In Seoul she became a kindergarten teacher at the Catholic school where she'd met a young priest named Joe. A virgin in her late twenties, she'd thought of becoming a nun, but Joe had convinced her not to.

"Joe opened my heart," she'd told me. "I'd feared men because of my father and my older step-brother, and my two younger half-brothers. Joe was so kind and gentle. We fell in love and I became pregnant. He was going to leave the priesthood to marry me, but I lost the child.

"I saw it as a sign from God that Joe was meant to be a priest. He is such a good man. I vowed that if he remained a priest, I would never marry. I kept that promise till I met you. Joe may have opened my heart, but you have stolen it forever."

I heard her voice telling me this again as if she were still alive and we were dancing together on New Year's Eve. Then I noticed that her dresser drawer was open; she'd taken a bound notebook from it and left it spread open on top of the dresser. I kissed her forehead and eased her head back onto the satin pillow. I went to the dresser and read the notebook where she'd printed very concisely, obviously some time ago. There was Father Joe's address and phone number in upstate New York, and she'd written that he had her last will and testament as well as her instructions and the funds to pay for her Catholic funeral and cremation. Her note read:

Joe will know what to do when you call him. He knows I love you and that I always will. Please be kind to him. He will grieve for me as much as you. Don't mourn for me forever. Spread your love. Others will need it. I will be waiting for you. Until then, you know what to do. Sarangeeyo yang han wee, I love you forever. Para XOX

I hung my head and wept. I took a deep breath and slammed the heel of my fist on the top of the dresser. The impact shook the dresser and the floppy-eared rabbit sitting on top of it began to gyrate. I gasped for breath as the maudlin melody of "Auld Lang Syne" poured into our bedroom like smoke from smoldering cinders.

My feet felt like lead with each belabored step toward the bed. I lifted Para into my arms. Her bare feet dangled in the air as we swayed to the music as if it were New Year's Eve in Times Square and the ball had dropped amid shouts of "Happy New Year!"

I would put off calling Father Joe until tomorrow. Meanwhile Para and I would continue to dance till dawn, me in black tie, she in her black chemise.

THE END

Romance Novel
Nancy Young

"IT'S NORA ROBERTS THIS week," Caitlyn reassured her father.

"Actual Nora Roberts? Not J. D. Robb?"

She could hear his anxiety twanging like a stretched rubber band through her cell phone.

"Actual Nora Roberts, Dad. She's still rereading the bride series." Caitlyn used her free hand to search the rack at Urban Outfitters, pausing to check the size on a promising red tee.

"Thank God. Life's hell when it's a J. D. Robb. She refuses to cook and wears that damn leather jacket." Mike Dixon's voice had dropped back to its bass level. "Thanks for the update, honey. And for keeping an eye on her. You know how she gets."

"Always glad to help, Daddy." She doubted her father sensed the sarcasm. "You won't have it easy, though. The bride series has serious implications. And it's tight skirts and extra makeup instead of leather these days." It was only fair to give him a heads-up this time around.

"I miss that year of Jane Austen, don't you?"

"I don't know, Dad. It got a little dull. She's more fun when she's into the contemporaries." Caitlyn moved on to the sale rack and considered a low-backed maxi dress.

"Easier to talk to, anyway. Think she's ready to see me?"

"They're wearing parkas in the underworld these days?" She rifled through the sundresses.

"It's been over a week."

"Considering you've been married for twenty-five years and eight days, a week isn't a whole lot of time."

"A week was all it took to know Laurie was the girl for me."

Caitlin let her exasperation seep into her reply. "Maybe you should tell her that."

"I know. I messed up. You don't have to keep reminding me."

"'Messed up' doesn't come close, Dad. That's like the captain of the Titanic saying he miscalculated." As Caitlyn's voice rose, two shoppers sidled over to the shoe section.

"I sent flowers as soon as I realized. Daisies. She likes daisies. I'm pretty sure. Or maybe it's those other puffy ones with the long name. Cris-something."

"Chrysanthemums? Dad, she's allergic to chrysanthemums."

"Then daisies were good?" Mike sounded a little desperate.

"Maybe she'll weave them into your funeral wreath. The way she's talking now, the only way she wants to see you is if you're in a box."

"City life has made you hard, Caity-did," Mike said. "So I go over the bridge and stay on 14th Street, right?"

"You got it." Caitlyn had reached the end of her patience and fallen off the edge. "Listen, Dad, I've got to go. I'm supposed to meet Mom outside the Botanic Garden in half an hour."

"See, I told you she likes flowers."

"Yeah, right. Call me once you think you're ready to come over. If I were you, I'd consider wearing a flak jacket." She was only partly kidding. She'd spent the last week with her mother, who was open to anything but reconciliation. Dutiful daughter that she was, Caitlin had carted them both downtown to the National Gallery, the Eastern Market, and even the drag queen brunch, where Laurie had downed three mimosas in quick succession as she watched the floor show. But enough was enough. It was time for Mom and Dad to kiss and make up so Caitlyn could get her life back.

***

The orchid room was steamy, and the waxy blooms reminded Laurie Dixon unpleasantly of her senior prom. Mike had worn a white dinner jacket that was two inches short in the sleeves and a blue tux shirt that exactly matched his eyes. His hands had shaken when he'd pinned the corsage to her bodice. As the evening wore on, the heavy flower sagged, bruising with each slow dance, until it was finally crushed flat in the backseat of his father's Olds while they'd lost their virginity together. She'd kept the ribbon pressed inside her leather-bound copy of *Pride and Prejudice*.

She thought she'd toss it when she went home to clear out her things.

Glancing at her phone, she noted she still had about half an hour to kill before her daughter was due. The humid conservatory was already making her hair curl. She didn't want to be all sweaty when they went to lunch. Thinking the air might be cooler in the garden court on the north side, she wove her way through the jungle plants, some of which looked disturbingly phallic, especially a bulging red anthurium. When she finally emerged in the outer conservatory, she was hotter than ever. A nearby bench beckoned—the perfect spot to calm down and read until Caitlyn found her.

With a contented sigh, Laurie pulled out her paperback and returned to the world of wedding planners in search of true love. The expected Sassy Heroine was closing in on her Mr. Right, surrounded by the lush bridal bouquets and elaborate decorations she created for a living. There were, of course, the Usual Complications, including the requisite Big Misunderstanding, but those were sure to be dispatched with a speed and ease Laurie wished were possible in real life. And when she read as far as the climactic kiss, it was heated enough to wilt blooms on their stalks and make her squirm on the hard bench.

The novel's heroine was as lush and dewy as her blossoms, and all the men swarmed around her like aphids on a rose. Laurie sat up a little straighter and tried crossing her legs so she'd look lush. Maybe if she puffed out her chest. Soon she gave up in discomfort after intercepting an uneasy glance from a German tourist.

So what if she was overblown instead of in her budding prime? It wasn't like she was ready for dead-heading. Pruning, maybe. Or color, she thought, reaching a hand up to touch the boring brown waves, graying near her ears. How would she look with raven tresses like the woman in the novel? No man could forget her then—lush Laura, the lily of the valley, a veritable Scarlett O'Hara of the suburbs. She saw herself turning heads in Crabtree Valley Mall as she sashayed down the central staircase without tripping or dropping her purse. The daydream held her until Caitlyn collected her for lunch.

***

Mike's stomach was growling by the time he headed around Thomas Circle for the second time, trying to make the turn onto Rhode Island Avenue. He hated DC—hated the tall buildings and pushy pedestrians and annoying one-way streets. He particularly hated traffic circles. That he was there in the nation's capital at all ought to prove to Laurie how much she meant to him. She should be grateful to be rescued from this place.

Just a week ago, he'd been trekking across vast Alpine fields in the Smokies, where tiny pink flowers poked through the grass and mountains rose like thunderclouds in the distance. He'd followed the spine of the park along the Appalachian Trail, skirting the state line that divided North Carolina from Tennessee. The trail crossed a road only once in seventy-one miles. And forget about cell phone service.

It had been great until he realized what day it was.

Seeing a gap open between a minivan and a Lexus, Mike ignored the chorus of horns and slid his sedan in, finally managing to escape from that circle of big city hell. Just one more turn and he'd be at the hotel. He hoped there was a bar. He needed a beer.

***

"Maybe a glass of wine?" Laurie toyed with the possibility as she looked up from the trendy menu and smiled brightly at her only child.

"Mom, it's barely noon. What's gotten into you?"

"I'm thinking of getting my hair done." She looked at herself reflected in the plate glass window—at her lackluster hair, pale gray eyes, and unremarkable features. Nothing about her stood out except maybe a few stubborn curls that stood up on top of her head, making her look like Cindy Lou Who. "I need a new color. Maybe black."

Caitlyn's mouth opened, but no sound came out. "What?"

"You don't think black suits me?"

"I think you'd look like Marilyn Manson."

"There's no need to be cruel, Caitlyn."

Caitlyn cocked her head. "How about starting with a modern cut—something that doesn't scream soccer mom."

At that, Laurie sat up even straighter. "I look like a soccer mom?"

"Only the cut. And you could add some highlights, sort of do it gradually—"

"But I want a big change."

"Mom, trust me. Change your shoes, paint your nails, enroll in a yoga class, but for big changes, stay away from your hair. Remember the last time I did mine?"

Laurie smiled fondly. "Such a pretty shade of orange. Like Annie."

"I was trying for smoking red."

"It was red for a little while."

"See, that's the thing about change, Mom. It looks good at first, but then it can turn into something really bad." Caitlyn paused for effect.

"Are we still talking about hair, Caity? Because if not, I think I'll order that glass of chablis."

"If you're serious about dyeing your hair, I can hook you up with my friend Stephanie this afternoon. She does hair and stuff." Caitlyn grinned. "Normal, attractive hair, Mom. We could even go for a mani and a pedi before."

"Don't you have to have long nails for that?" Laurie looked at her hands. They were practical hands, accustomed to gardening and dishwashing and typing. Hands that had changed this kid's diapers. Hands that used to reach for Mike each night.

"Well, you can get long nails if you want, or you can just shape and color what you have and enjoy being pampered." Caitlyn's smile widened.

Laurie had a flash of herself scraping long red nails down an anonymous muscular back. "Long nails it is," she grinned, flushing, and for a moment the two women looked like mirror images, one sharp, one blurry. She was due for some pampering, darn it. A makeover was the perfect place to start.

***

"Just perfect," Mike muttered when he learned he'd have to wait two hours to check in, plus he'd have to pay for parking. At least the clerk could point him to the bar. Now he really needed that cold beer and a sandwich chock full of cholesterol to go with it. There were advantages to not having Laurie looking over his shoulder.

He'd left the toilet seat up all week, for instance. And had hot dogs for dinner. Watched all four games Saturday. And . . . He was having trouble coming up with the other advantages, but he knew there were plenty.

Life had seemed so simple a week ago—just the trail, the wildlife, and him. He'd lost track of the days on the switchbacks and balds, ducking under deadfalls and tripping over rocks. He'd count his steps when the trail got rough—a thousand steps to the next plateau, eight thousand before lunch. But when the trail was easy along the ridge, he'd let himself think. Not about the next project or what the stock market was doing or reseeding the lawn. And what he thought bothered him. Because out there, on the open trail, for the first time in a long time he didn't feel trapped.

His life was great—successful career, nice house, comfortable marriage. He had it all, didn't he? So why did he have the feeling that he needed something more? More excitement. More adventure. More of a sense that he was the quarterback instead of a linebacker. As he argued with himself, he'd kept his eyes on the trail, watching for roots, counting the steps to the next white blaze. Most of the time he walked alone, though at night he shared the shelters with mice and through-hikers.

It's not like he was seeing another woman.

Bad weather and all that thinking took a toll on his daily mile count, so he'd reached his endpoint a day late. He winced as he remembered the exact moment he realized what date it was and how many miles still stretched between himself and home.

And Laurie.

It had taken a while to get a signal, but she didn't pick up when he called. At the first town he came to he'd stopped at a florist's and ordered flowers. He was pretty sure they were daisies, something happy-looking and bright, like the wildflowers he'd walked through. He'd asked the salesgirl to put a rush on the order and had taken the time to fill out the card: *Happy Anniversary, honey—better late than never!! All my love.* But when he finally pulled in the garage late that night, he'd found the flowers in the trash, the dog boarded at the vet, and Laurie gone.

He didn't feel trapped anymore, that's for damn sure. Mike Dixon was a guy with a mission: get back what he'd had. Because it's only when you lose it that you understand the thing that trapped you was really holding you up all along.

Mike finished the beer without realizing it as he planned his strategy. He'd put on those gray slacks she was always trying to get him to wear and greet her with a five-second kiss. Then he'd take her out for a thick steak. He'd apologize. Then they'd go back to the fancy hotel room he'd just rented and rumple the sheets up good before he drove her home where she belonged. Smiling, he left a hefty tip on the table. He was looking forward to that first kiss.

***

"Sun-kissed," Stephanie nodded.

"Not too brassy?" Laurie asked nervously, fingering the newly-brightened strands.

"Mom, you wanted change. You got change. And it's cute."

"I was going for seductive." Laurie tried out a sultry look in the mirror above the vanity but gave up when Stephanie stifled a giggle. Maybe seductive was out of her league. She might have to settle for well-groomed.

Caitlyn patted her shoulder. "It's just hair, Mom. You can't expect too much. Did you bring along your red dress?"

Stephanie jumped on the cheerleading squad. "You really do look great. This cut makes your eyes look bigger, and the color brightens up your complexion."

Laurie tried not to think about how bad she must have looked in the before picture. No wonder Mike hadn't remembered their anniversary. She was totally forgettable. Her lips started to quiver and her unsultry, beady little eyes filled with tears.

Caitlyn and Stephanie exchanged glances. "So, Mom, um, where should we go for dinner this time? A grill? A bistro? Pizza?"

Her daughter's voice sounded way too hearty, like a coach trying to rally the team after a disappointing first half. The football analogy tackled her unawares, pushing her back to the line of scrimmage and to Mike, who'd probably spent all day Saturday in his recliner drinking beer and watching game after game. That image gave her the impetus she needed to sit up and get on with creating a new Laurie. *Change is good*, she reminded herself. *Be the change.* She repeated it like a mantra.

"Mom?"

"Ethiopian," Laurie stated emphatically. "I passed a place on U Street."

Caitlyn raised her freshly threaded eyebrows. "Have you ever actually eaten Ethiopian?"

Wasn't her daughter supposed to be supporting her in this effort? "That's why we should have some tonight. Change is good."

"It's spicy. And you might have to sit on the floor. And eat with your fingers," Caitlyn warned.

"I'm not so decrepit that I can't get up off the floor, and I'm sure they have napkins. And as for spicy—I want some spice in my life." Maybe not cayenne pepper, but a nice rich cinnamon would certainly make her bland world more interesting, she thought. More appealing. Less lonely.

***

Mike's stride was wide as he passed Meridian Hill Park and waited out the traffic on Sixteenth Street so he could cross over to his daughter's building. The trees in the park were just starting to leaf out. New start, new life. By tonight, his own life would be back on track, especially after he convinced Laurie to try out the king-size bed in that overpriced boutique hotel. He paused, feet apart, looking up at the apartment window where his wife and daughter waited. He felt like king of the hill.

While Caitlin fussed with her flat iron, Laurie looked herself up and down in the mirror on the back of the door. Her red dress clashed a bit with the hair, and she'd better not eat much if she wanted the waist to fit after dinner. "Change is good," she repeated softly, trying to get used to the four-inch heels she'd borrowed.

"No sign of rain, right?" Caitlyn called as she picked up her bag. Laurie parted the curtains to check the sidewalk two stories down. Teetering unsteadily, arms crossed, she turned to her daughter.

"Caitlyn Marie, there appears to be a man with a bald spot down there who's staring up at your window. I'd call the police if I were you."

"Come on, Mom. Cut the poor guy a break. He drove all the way up here to see you.

"I always knew you were a daddy's girl." Irritation and an uncomfortable edginess sharpened her voice.

"I'm a mommy's girl too. That's why I gave him directions. Come on. Be nice."

"I'm always nice, damn it." She hid behind the curtain so Mike wouldn't see her watching.

"No, you're not. Nice is not smiling like you're planning to bite somebody. Let's go down and meet him so he doesn't get stuck in the elevator."

"Is there a real chance of that?" Laurie brightened at the prospect.

"Come along, Mother."

Idly waiting in the driveway till his girls came out, Mike noticed the curvy blonde as soon as she came off the elevator. She was a walking invitation in those heels. For a full thirty seconds he watched in appreciation as she wiggled through the lobby and out the glass door. Then his belly dropped to the pavement. That wasn't just some good-looking woman. That was Laurie. Clearing his throat, he forced a cheerful look on his face. "Hey, honey." His voice sounded high to him.

Laurie managed to stay cool, despite the concentrated effort it took to stand upright in the shoes.

"Hello, Mike. Fancy meeting you here in civilization." She thought her voice hit the right level of indifferent sophistication.

Mike felt the frostbite, and his smile froze. Still, what did he expect? He'd known he'd have to thaw her a bit to get her to come home. He guessed the kiss was a no-go.

"I have to admit the city has at least one attraction. You look great."

"Nice of you to notice." Laurie was proud of the offhand tone. Where was Caitlyn? Traitorous little brat. Laurie glanced over her shoulder as casually as she could without losing her balance. Caitlyn was slinking out of the lobby door.

"So, fam, are we ready to eat?" Caitlyn ignored her mother's icy glare.

"You bet," her dad said with more enthusiasm than the occasion called for. "Where's the nearest steak house?"

"Mom already picked out the restaurant, Dad. Consider it an adventure."

***

Mike looked down at the round platter dotted with globs of what he supposed was food—red globs, a bright green glob, a glob with what looked like corn in it, and another that looked like something the dog threw up. He ordered another beer. At least he'd convinced them to sit in a booth.

Laurie was doing her best to seem at ease, but he knew the signs. She kept hitching her neckline up and fixing her straps, and every few minutes she took another sip of water. Caitlyn was trying to ignore the tension, digging into the pools of stuff in front of her and tossing conversation openers.

"So, Dad, how's business?"

Mike felt on firm ground here. "Just brought on a new account. Should keep me plenty busy for the next month or so."

Laurie remained studiedly disinterested.

"Mom, how's your book?"

"Oh, I'm about halfway through. They're past the kiss and into the complications."

"Don't you ever get tired of them? They all sound kind of the same."

"They are not!" Laurie set down her water glass. "This one's all about wedding planning—the flowers, the cake, everything that goes into making the day special." She took a breath. "And who could ever get tired of romance?"

Mike knew he was the target for that missile.

"You should read some real books, Mom. The stuff you read could never happen. Most people just hook up. And nobody gets married anymore."

Laurie caught herself meeting Mike's eyes. "Maybe that's because people just don't care like they used to." When she leaned forward, Mike did his best to keep his eyes from drifting to her neckline. It had been a long couple of weeks.

"Once you love someone, you're both changed forever." Laurie's voice trembled slightly. "It's like taming a stray. You can't just forget it once it's yours. You become responsible forever for what you tame."

"Sounds like crap to me," Mike shifted in his seat. "People aren't stray dogs, for Christ sake."

"'*Tu es responsable de ta rose*,'" Laurie whispered.

"Say what?"

Caitlyn looked up from the chickpeas. "It's French, Daddy."

"It's a quote from one of those *real* books we liberal arts majors had to read instead of romance novels. *Le Petit Prince*. Antoine de Saint-Exupéry." Laurie paused. "Not the kind of book you would know. No spies and submarines."

"Anyone want coffee?"

Shaking her head at Caitlyn's chirpy attempt to cut the tension, Laurie folded her napkin and dropped a twenty on the table. "It feels a little stuffy in here. I'll see you back at the apartment, Caity." She mustered as much grace as she could and got to the door before the tears leaked out.

"What the hell was she talking about now?" Mike felt like he'd landed in the Twilight Zone, and everybody knew the secret but him.

"It's a book, Dad."

Mike's expression remained clueless.

"Barnes and Noble is open until ten on Saturdays," Caitlin offered. "It's just over on Twelfth. Get a translation."

***

In the patch of morning sun near a spray of orchids, Laurie settled onto the bench she thought of as hers and opened her novel to the last chapter. She was determined to lose herself in the story and let go of the jumbled feelings that had kept her awake most of the night on Caitlyn's sofa.

Mike had looked tired. And thinner. Not that she cared. No, she didn't care at all. She was a changed woman now. What more could she need than a room full of flowers and a book? She was about to get to the best part, when the intrepid heroine and her perfect alpha male had finally untangled their plot twists and were about to unite in a happily ever after.

Somehow, it all seemed stale and silly today.

Despite her vow to focus on her book, snippets of memory crept in—Mike at dinner, peeling the label off his beer, Mike dunking her in the lake when they were teens, Mike holding his daughter for the first time, Mike sitting by her side at her mother's funeral, Mike stopping the car last month and picking her a bunch of daisies growing at the side of a country road.

Mike.

***

He inched his sedan past the Capitol, cursing the mobs that clogged the crosswalk even after the light had changed. All of Washington was in gridlock. He slammed his hand against the steering wheel and gritted his teeth. On the other side of the dome, he could see the conservatory, just as Caitlyn had described it, a giant cage of glass and steel. Almost there. He had to make his move. Ignoring signs and the likelihood of a ticket, he pulled into a vacant space in a restricted lot to his left and headed east at a lope, hunting for his wife. No camo today though. He'd dressed with care in his best navy-blue suit and a tie she'd given him a few years ago, back when he still wore ties to work.

Time to wake up and smell the roses, he thought ruefully as he cut across the grass.

***

Restless, Laurie slapped her book shut and pushed to the center of the clammy courtyard, crowded today with what looked like a seniors' garden club outing. On the other side of the stone path, she watched an octogenarian sink onto a wall and wave his wife on. She shook her head and settled her ample bottom in the space next to him.

Laurie's chest hurt. Turning her back on the couple, she squeezed her hips onto a ledge between two planters packed with elephant ears. The air around her seemed too thick and sweet. Her cotton skirt snagged on an overgrown quince, scattering petals at her feet. She stared at them until all she could see were blurred pink dots. She had to leave. Now. Before she broke down in front of all these nice old people.

It took her two tries to untangle her flowing white skirt from the stubborn branch. She ended up ripping a hole in the fabric before she freed herself. Purse over her shoulder, novel under her arm, she dodged mothers pushing strollers, tourists with cameras on tripods, and another clump of elderly flower enthusiasts.

As she pushed past a gurgling fountain, someone grabbed her hand, the one that still wore the gold band she couldn't tug over her knuckle. She knew that touch, knew who held her before she turned around. She looked down at their joined hands, noticing how her red nails poked like firecrackers from between his fingers. Ridiculous. And yet, her hand so easily adjusted, fitting the contours of his out of habit.

She raised her eyes.

His were what had drawn her all those years ago, eyes the color of forget-me-nots and a steady gaze that made her hot and shivery at the same time. That was back when he was a gangly teenager, lean and wiry, with a heart-tugging half grin. Then, the look in his eyes was all it took for her to bang through the screen door and run to the driveway where he waited in his dented Chevy, Springsteen blaring on the radio. The way he'd looked at her made her ache, made her want to slide over, straddle the stick shift, and climb all over him.

When he'd looked at her, back then when they were young and love was real, she'd shifted gears out of idle and up through third, then fourth, engine racing.

He was looking at her now. The man in front of her was broader, his hair was thinner, and his eyes crinkled in the greenhouse sun. But the look in them hadn't changed.

"*Je suis responsable de ma rose,*" he said in horrible French, learned courtesy of the internet. Nodding at the flower hanging over her shoulder, he added, "Even with the thorns." His eyes locked her in place. But, of course, she'd lost the will to run.

"That's a hibiscus." Laurie's smile was shaky. So were her legs, but the pressure on her chest had eased.

"Do you always have to be right?" He slid his warm hand up and down her bare arm. She shivered.

"It just works out that way most of the time." Laurie could feel a flush rise. She didn't think it was a hot flash.

Mike had to look away from the open want on her face or he'd embarrass them both. His eyes focused on the label beneath some orange-red flower in the border. *Floribunda. Impatient.* "Once when I was hiking, I came out of the trees into a clearing. It was pretty late in the afternoon, and I still had a mile to go before I hit the shelter. But there was this patch of weeds that looked almost like it was on fire. The sun was just starting to go down behind it." He cleared his throat. "It was the same color as your hair. The color it used to be. Kind of golden." He reached a hand to her curls. "Sort of like our first dog. Beautiful."

"The dog?"

"He was a great dog," he smiled. "But you know what I mean."

"I always know what you mean, Mike. I just want to hear you say it." Laurie waited, willing him to change.

Mike made an effort not to look away this time. "Whenever I'm hiking, and I see something like a field of wildflowers or a chipmunk or a hawk riding a thermal, the first thing I think is how much you'd love that." His brows drew down when she didn't respond. "Hell, Laurie, I'm sorry I was late. I'm sorry that I didn't make it back in time for our anniversary. But even when I'm gone, I take you with me." He closed the distance between them in one step. "Come home. Come back with me." He raised her hand to his lips, red nails and all.

Laurie held her breath, afraid that if she let it go, the moment would be lost. It was the same feeling she had when she was on the last page of a novel, savoring the exquisite moment before shutting the book.

While a line of ladies raised their brows, she ran her hands up Mike's starched shirt and hooked her arms around his neck. The paperback fell to the ground.

"Take me now," she whispered, her voice husky and gaze sultry enough for a place on the erotica shelf.

And despite the onlookers, Mike pulled her against him, bent his head, and kissed her— kissed her until the fertile air was thick with thrumming and throbbing and sighing, but stopping just short of bodice ripping, in deference to the astounded crowd.

Otherwise occupied, Laurie never noticed her battered paperback on the floor. And when she left with Mike, the novel found its resting place next to the fountain, beside a flame-red rose.

THE END

Flash Fiction

In a Castle in France

Julia Ballerini

ONCE UPON A TIME in a castle in France, a man locked his wife in a tower upon learning she had a lover. She lived alone for forty years save for a trusted servant who brought her frugal meals. Apart from a narrow bed, her room was bare.

In a moment of pity, the dishonored husband granted her one request. She asked for paints and brushes. So it came to pass that on the gray walls of her cell grew lush green fields sprinkled with red poppies flourishing beneath blue skies flecked with white clouds.

Only after her death did the secret heart of her artistry come to light: her bed upturned, its wooden underside revealed a full-bodied portrait of her lover, his bare, young arms reaching to embrace the hard surface on which she had lain those forty years.

Night Owl
Guy Biederman

CARMEN SLEEPS UNTIL ONE in the afternoon and eats breakfast for dinner at four. When her neighbor Cleve arrives home from his work, she's just getting started with hers. He hears her moving around in the flat upstairs, a ball rolling across the wooden floor followed by the cat in pursuit, then her voice. Carmen hums as she paints and in the sounds she makes, he sees color. He coughs. She stops. They listen to the sounds of evening—the frogs in the pond, a distant bird of prey. He smokes and stays up way too late for his delivery job that starts at dawn.

The cat finds something, a pipe cleaner. Another life-and-death struggle ensues. And when the cat pounces and pauses, the pipe cleaner gripped in its paws, Carmen resumes her humming and Cleve falls asleep, metallic purple pulsing in his mind.

She paints through the night, the cat fast asleep, Cleve lightly snoring downstairs—inspiring strokes of yellow against the purple canvas of the night. Her upstairs light casts a small glow on the ground below, where his pickup waits for morning.

Six Word Stories

The expensive fragrance revitalized her skin.
Heide Arbitter

One dance, nothing more required.
Kirk Beeler

Two soloists sang duets, became trio.
Elizabeth Cockle

Say you love me. For now.
R.B. Frank

Souls embrace, bodies mingle, love abides.
Michel Krug

For sale: Lover's toothbrush. Best offer.
Cindy Matthews

Without you, all connection is lost.
Phyllis McKinley

I loved him by the wedding.
Mattie Lee Monroe

Share your words, share your love!
Valerie J. Runyan

She, my sentence. I, her parentheses.
Jeffrey H. Toney

Her withheld embrace stored wondrous fulfillment.
Gerald Winter

Two distinct mother tongues, one kiss.
Marlene Woods

Poetry

Infinite

Margaritë Camaj

One
To love one man with all of my being
With all of my soul
With all that I have
So deeply that we have each other's heart
Without possession
To go to the darkest parts of your soul
Where none had the courage to stay and love
Until he has found that I am his missing piece
To show the world that love isn't as weak as
they make it seem
And that it defeats anything that goes against it
Not riches
Not degrees
Not anything material
Just love
One man
One woman
One
This was always enough
This was always my definition of success

The Cleanse

I will not give you hell,
not even for a second
Hell lives there, not here
I told you I was not them
I am me
And, in the rain, I will
show you what heaven looks like,
washing your sins into poetry

Flawed

I have no desire for a man to think that I am perfect
None
I never did
If he thinks that, for one second, then that means
that he doesn't know the pain that I hold
The way that there are nights that I breathe a little
too difficult
Or when my heart starts to beat too fast for my own body
to handle
Or the way my thoughts consume me, whole
He is incapable of seeing that I am human,
and with that comes imperfections that are at times too
deep for
the human mind and heart to even understand
I have no desire for a man to ever think I am perfect
I will repeat this until my lungs no longer allow me
to breathe
For if he does, he doesn't know me,
and that will never turn into love
Love knows all the corners of you,
even the darkest ones

Amore

Hannah Fields

Here's to all the right lovers
appearing on my doorstep
at exactly the wrong time.
All these memorable ghosts
pervade my reverie on a dime.

I lift my glistening glass to you,
the man with knowing ocean eyes
who taught me to love so freely
through charcoal lines of poetry
we passed late into the night.

Here's to the hopeless romantics
with all their far-fetched dreams
dotted with forever and wedding rings.
I'm sorry they could never quite see
why their love just wasn't for me.

I propose a toast to you,
my favorite whirlwind romance
and all the plans we dared to make
knowing they'd never have a chance
in this game of curious happenstance.

Here's to the unfinished kisses
left upon the lips of wanting men,
brevity forming question marks
where answers failed to begin
signaling preludes to an end.

I steadily drink to you,
my faceless fabled suitor
destined to change it all,
yet, I won't sit here waiting
to answer your honeyed beck and call.

And Still I Love You More

Elise Holland

The tide at its highest.
The gravitational pull
of a love-struck ocean
to a thirsty shore,
driven
by the sun and the moon.
The love affair
between the pen and the paper.
Blackened pages rich
with the art they've created.
Elizabeth Bennet and Mr. Darcy,
Tristan and Isolde.
The rush of conviction
shown by the present,
as it hurls itself
toward its beloved future
where together,
we will shape memories
yet to be revealed.
And still I love you more.

Love and Romance

Mother's Day Poem
Michel Krug

Some kisses are instant, purified
Instants . . . with complex flavors
Of marriage, of overwhelming
Affection, taste and the scent of years
That build and soften like warm
Wind that modulates and doesn't stop.

Other kisses still jump and probe
Descending into sultry memories restored
With a certain sense of imbalance when its
Immensity is not fully correspondent.

When the summer air simmers
Our skin welcomes the ambiance
When it's so quiet in the house
That your breath is
The only wind and the night sky
Glows through the window
From a mountainous full moon
That reflects onto you
At that moment, you are akin to
A mother by nature
And so I want to be one with you.

Love Rhyme

Deeply	stored
Love has a	core
Our body of	lore
Once another's love	pours
Its lustrous gown	worn
Mutuality to	explore
In encore after	encore.

I Love:

The way she seats her trunk so strong
Her core and arms in rhythm with the wind
The natural designs of her perforated
Colors shining glossy then matte in the sun.

The way the planes glide effortlessly
Through the air, tricking distance
And time, displacement of life
To engage a taste of galactic travel

The way the crocuses fight through
Ice and promise perfectly contoured
Rows of spring hidden behind a peel of
Winter that yields to a longing April

When the way the fresh cut grass so
Tender and still soft as it adjusts to
Carpet and insert green atop the former gray so
White lines are drawn, where fair balls bounce.

The way the spring reveals the truth about
Rebirth and the possibility that the greed of
Cold can be vanquished when informed
Consensus weather's past, feigned ignorance

The way a dynasty of lies is debunked
And we touch in brief moments of harmony
In belief and festival, in art, in heart
Until another calamity tests our love.

And the way she holds me and I her
Amid the dizziness of daily life
Which promises regularity but spins
Doubts that ultimately wither to love itself.

Barstools and Nightstands

Refill
David Lukas

You made me coffee in the morning.
It was terrible,
some of the worst I've ever had
but you were proud of yourself
and sat down at the kitchen table
wearing nothing
to watch me drink it.
I pretended to like it
even though it washed away
the taste of you
still on my tongue
I was saving for the train ride home.
When I was finished
I untied my shoes
and stayed two more nights
to get the taste of your terrible coffee
out of my mouth.

Window Shopping

I left the bookstore empty handed
because of the couple
standing in front of the book I wanted

Fiction
Last Names C-E

I don't know
if they are an actual couple
or if they see each other on weekdays
but they were laughing and whispering
and probably would have been kissing too
if I wasn't in the aisle
pretending to look for another book
hoping they would leave.

I let them keep the book I wanted—
two lovers have the right of way
even if they have no business
in a bookstore

Fiction
Last Names C-E

Are You Still Watching?

I cringe when I hear couples
talk about *our show*
the one they never miss
and spend whole weekends
watching entire seasons.
The only thing you should be binging
is each other,
too addicted to pay attention
to anything else shown on a screen,
unable to stop a Friday kiss goodbye
from turning into a three-day bender
holed up in bed
no clothes, no food, no sleep
begging for just

one more, one more, one more

until you're engulfed
and she's in your hair
on your lips
under your fingernails
so strong
that you close your tired eyes

and return to her arms
every time you take a sip of coffee
to keep yourself awake
with all the other strung out addicts
at Port Authority
while you wait for the last bus home
on a Sunday night.

B Bar

You threw a half-empty bottle
just above my head
trying to drown me
in a sea of broken glass—
cheap drunk
cheap fight
cheap walls,
it went right through.
We couldn't help but laugh
and that's how that one ended:
up against the wall
drinking your cheap red wine.

Extra Credit

In school I took a course
called Exploring The Universe
but we never left the classroom
and the professor reduced supernovas and millennia
to bullet points
and uniform, little circles on a Scantron.
So I stopped going
and for my final project submitted
a collection of poems inspired by the stars
the last one was Whitman's
the one about perfect silence.
My professor was not amused
D-
Everyone talked about how easy that class was
but later there was a meteor shower
at three in the morning
and I noticed no one else
lying in the grass
behind the baseball fields
except the girl
breathing wine and warmth down my neck.

I have explored the universe
but prefer the view from down here.

Love Poem

My dad used to drink Manhattans
when I was little.
I looked up at him
and imagined the entire city
shining in his glass.
Outside I'd cup the skyline in my hands
and pretend to drink it too.

Now I hold the real thing
in a bar off Broadway
wishing this city did fit in one glass
so I could drink it down
every last drop
until there's nothing left
but a hangover.

A Love Letter to Me

My Own Sun
Francesca Lupini

He used to write poems comparing me to the moon;
a bright light in the darkness,
a beam of goodness.
I was unfiltered happiness,
moonlight guiding him through
the unknown.
At the time,
his metaphors about my eyes
being celestial orbs seemed to be
the most romantic sentiment I'd ever receive.
But then I wrote my own love poem,
dedicated to me;
I decided against my being his moon,
but became my own sun.
For no longer will I rely on someone else to illuminate me;
my light comes from within.

Yellow Rain Boots

She was yellow rain boots
walking calmly through a thunderstorm.
With rain rushing down around her,
she remained herself,
never letting the rain dampen her heart.
She remained warm, gentle, and real.
She was the depth in her dark eyes,
she was the softness in her voice when she asked
far too often if you were okay.
She was simple,
a rare beauty no one could question.
She was nothing you've ever known, but
everything you ever wanted.
Yet you let her walk away
through the rain,
yellow rain boots and all.

Solitary

I am my most beautiful
in moments nobody has ever seen before.
In my most private moments,
when my inner thoughts emerge,
and enter reality through ink.
I am most beautiful when I am
broken,
torn up by my own words.
Deep in thought,
chewing on my pen,
creating,
that is when I have the most potential.
I am most beautiful when I have power,
when I can create my own reality on paper,
when I am in control.
I am my best
alone.

Discounted Artwork

A boy once told me I was a work of art;
he claimed my body curved in the right spots
and that my smile was delicately
painted to perfection.
He said I was a masterpiece:
one of a kind and priceless.
But when we went to the art museum
that cold rainy day,
I saw through the facade of this overused compliment;
as I watched him overlook countless paintings,
discount works of art,
with a glazed look on his face,
I knew he did not understand the way
art makes one feel,
the sheer power of the brush stroke.
So surely,
he cannot truly understand the masterpiece that I am.

Dawn

I was awake before the sun today.
I lay awake, restless, until the light began
softly shining in my window,
tainted by the city lights and smog.
The room was illuminated,
the color of your eyes,
a soft hazy blue.
The sunrise danced softly on my skin,
light and playful,
like your hand used to brush against my bare legs
on late nights and sleepy mornings.
The world is silent,
I am alone,
and although you're missed,
although you still linger in my mind
in beautiful moments like this,
I am okay.

My Favorite Color

I never had a favorite color
before now.
Before I saw the color of your eyes
reflected in my morning cup of coffee,
I had no idea that brown could be
someone's favorite color.
Before I met you,
I never realized how incomplete
my world would be without
brown.
No trunks for trees,
no leather for my boots,
no you.
No breathless brown eyes,
no cinnamon tan skin,
nothing I know,
nothing I love
would be as it is without that
muddled shade of everything.
Brown.

Usual Desires

What I Want
Lisa St. John

I want . . . more than a red dress (I've had one or two).
I want severance pay for time served. Sloan Kettering can validate my parking.
I want the ends to justify the means, and I want healthy chocolate.

I want to rub the bottle of cabernet like a genie's lamp and watch you appear. You've traveled to stranger places.

I want to stop dreaming that you are still alive I want to never stop dreaming that you are still alive.

I want to sleep later and longer to shorten my time here—this place where you are not,
but were.

I want that sexy spot of in-between (when your leg shakes you almost awake but not quite) to last longer. This hypnagogic jerk is not as involuntary as it sounds.

I want people to stop asking me if I am ready to move . . . on.

Move like a pawn, a little at a time? Or like an elegant, sweeping queen across this black and white deathboard? Whether I move on or above or about or between, beyond, through, or underneath—I am still without.

No preposition of wanting will win this argument of time and place and space.

I want to stop
wanting.

Maybe Then

I want to die before the imprinted pads of paper run out,
your logo disappearing.
I hurry to finish painting the barn because maybe when it's
done I too can be done
and go.

But then there's the deck. I'm not sure what you would have
wanted me to do with that. Repair? Tear down and make new?

My anger and frustration are only quelled by hiding
the anger and frustration and
it takes a lot of energy. It takes a lot of work.

Maybe when I am brave enough to listen to your voice again .
. . the podcasts, the interviews—
maybe when I can at least
listen to your playlists (ever the DJ, you were).

Maybe then I can go.

Life is, indeed, very long, but I am more than hollow; I am
carved and crooked.

Maybe when I can stop noticing your favorite yellow finches
dining on purpled coneflowers—maybe if I can stop the tears
when the pinks of apple blossoms from your tree appear
and fall
and stick to the wet wooden porch swing, maybe when
September's soft beckoning breeze refuses to remind me of
your hand on my cheek—

maybe then.

Peter Pan's Madrigal

You were never meant to stay
rooted to the ground, or even to one country—let alone this
plane.
You had a Peter Pan shadow with luggage tag attached.

Grateful that you taught me (finally) how to play,
our story became one of life untamed.
You were never meant to stay
rooted to the ground, or even to one country—let alone this
plane.

Nothing you have given me can be taken away,
but nothing you have given me will ever be the same.
I know by some magic moving against the grain
that you were never meant to stay
rooted to the ground, or even to one country—let alone this
plane.
You had a Peter Pan shadow with luggage tag attached.

The Whens of Now

When the gloaming begins and the sky becomes a Turner painting,
when the air smells of fallen leaves and cut grass and the dog is tired from her run and the cats are just waking in a crepuscular mood, and crickets serenade the last of the fireflies—that now.

When hero-bats flood the dwindling horizon light and frogs are in a brief conclave with the sleepy bees,
when trees turn silhouette from the bottom up and when the product of technology and nature lovemaking blinks on

one by one in solared garden lights—

when just before the darkening oranges take over for their 15 seconds of fame and we could be in the Sedona Red Rocks or in a field of Van Gogh's Saint-Remy sunflowers,
when we sit on the rooftop in San Miguel de Allende drinking wine,

when, when, when this is now—if only for a moment. It was.

Oh, here comes the past tense again. Not yet.

There Are Dreams

There are dreams, my love,
I cannot dream without you.
There are colors, my lover,
I cannot see alone.

The nuances of this world—
The beauty and the kindness
Are hidden from me without your eyes,
And laughter has no music . . . only
the dull thud of an unwelcome awakening.

You told me once that the world was good.
But I didn't smell the bloom of sunrise or
hear the bellow of azure skies
until I felt through your essence—

The light of this
World.

Listen

Let them collapse like paper dolls in the rain, these fears.
Screams are not howls and not cries—all is echo,
echo of scavenged tears.

Mythologies transparent as jellyfish and just as deadly
writhe in the corners of our thoughts
if we allow them. Their sounds, a gruesome medley.

We gulp our madness down like shots
instead of sipping the bigger story.
This is how history plots.

But there is a tale ancient as breath
that whispers to us all.
In this version, the happily ever after is ours
if we can hear her song through clouded stars.

I Am Thirsty for You

At times it is like a milkshake craving, pure vanilla longing. Wanting to hop in the car with the windows down and summer wind blowing warm. Knowing the satisfaction waiting at the end—it is a calm, steady desire. Urgent only in the sense that an ice cream sandwich wouldn't come close. It has to be a milkshake. It has to be vanilla in a sweating paper cup while I bite the straw and suck hard.

Other times it is like the water so desperately needed in the middle of a hangover. The lifesaving liquid would go right into my aching brain cells and osmose itself through the alcohol membrane that's thick enough to lock my tongue to the roof of my mouth. The clear, cool feel of it down my scorched throat and, somehow, up into my howling bloody eyes, it saves me. It lets me lie down again and breathe deeply. It gives whatever nightmare creatures growing in my mouth a run for it. And I can sleep.

My thirst for you in the morning is like dark, thick Mexican coffee with cream. A languorous, dreamy desire full of strong soaking scent. A steaming, yet cautious yearning to sip and not get burned, but wanting it so badly it's hard not to try. The first taste bringing me out of the dream and into the smell of morning. The last swallow making me want to run to the store for newspapers and an egg sandwich. Satisfied.

So I question if I am a fizzy brown soda, dancing around your mouth in bubbles of excitement and cleansing. I could come with lemon if you like. Or am I a robust Chilean red wine, sliding down your throat in silky waves to warm your stomach?

I sometimes think I am an antacid waiting to be mixed; burbling so I can cure you.

But what I want to be is both your cold chocolate milk craving and your sweet morning juice.

Crush

I wonder if you are wearing that t-shirt—the one that is plain blue and non-descript and makes me want to rip it off of you, or, snuggle into it.
I wonder how it would feel on me—on my bare breasts, soft, against my raised hard nipples, enveloping me in scent-memory of you.

Looking for you in this sea of faces I wonder if you are looking for me, or at least thinking of me.

Because the fantasy of it is what turns us on; the craving of desire, the longing
to want . . . and be wanted. The flutter of passion, the need to yearn.

Pulses in my chest in my groin, aching to be right about this. Would I really do anything about it after all? I wonder.

Where is Ophelia's Mother?

Ophelia had her hands full when you
think about it. How many men can one
woman please? Daddy, lover, brother—too
much testosterone for a girl so young.

Who were her role models? Gertrude? Whore
or innocent, however you view her
she is black and white, and a girl needs more
shades to learn truth; that sisterlove is near.

Ophelia's frustrated voice is heard
centuries later, yet here we still drown.
Without the mother the lines are too blurred.
Remembering in wombs alive, girls born,
forgetting. Why can't we dream them stronger?
Where is her mother? Today, only anger.

How to Submit Your Short Fiction or Poetry to 2 Elizabeths

At 2 Elizabeths, we welcome both new and established writers, and we are pleased to consider work that has not yet been published. It is our goal to bring to light stories and poetry from well-known authors as well as from emerging voices, with dignity and respect.

Throughout the year we accept submissions of short fiction and poetry from writers all across the globe. In addition to our general submissions, we host various writing contests featuring cash prizes and publishing opportunities. You can obtain a full copy of our submission guidelines, including instructions for submitting your work, here:

bit.ly/2ESubmissionGuidelines.

About the 2E League

IF YOU'VE EVER WISHED for a strong writing community, we want the 2E League to be your hub. If you'd love to find beta-readers and/or critique partners to read your work, as well as have the opportunity to support other writers—we are your tribe.

Member Benefits

    * Private writing contests only open to 2E League members

    * An exclusive invitation to attend a networking call (held 3-4 times annually) with the editor of 2 Elizabeths and other members of the 2E League

    * Access to the 2E League private Facebook group where members can network, ask and answer questions, and find beta-readers and critique partners

    * Access to our private, members-only web page which features writing resources, private contest details, and a calendar of events

The 2E League is only open to new members a few select times during the year. Get more information and join our wait list here: bit.ly/2ELeagueWaitList.

About the Authors

Fiction

Catherine Brown

Catherine Brown is a writer whose poetry has been featured in *Oakwood*, the literary journal of South Dakota State University. Most recently, she was a runner-up in the 2016 flash fiction/prose poetry contest at *The Offbeat*, from Michigan State University. She is also a pharmacist, published in technical journals and a professional textbook. She has a passion for writing, animal rescue and conservation, and making jewelry. She lives with her husband and her cats in Renton, Washington. To learn more about Catherine, visit her website here: https://www.chbrownauthor.com/.

R.B. Frank

R.B. Frank has won short story contests and published several online and peer-reviewed articles, as well as a flash fiction/short story collection titled *Bite Size Reads*: *slightly twisted, deliciously dark, really short stories for people with very little time or really short attention spans*. She is currently working on her first love, picture books! She has two kids, two dogs, one husband and when she's not loving on them, she's worrying about them. You can find her at rbfrank.com, on Instagram @writingoutloud, or on Twitter @writingoutloud2.

James Magner, MD

James Magner, MD is a physician and scientist who has written many scientific publications, but is new to writing fiction. He is an endocrinologist and biochemist who for many years studied thyroid-stimulating hormone. He enjoys chess and poker, and he has appeared on ESPN during a major poker tournament. He met his wife, Glenda, at University of Chicago in a laundromat, and they raised two daughters. His humorous autobiography, *Free to Decide: Building a Life in Science and Medicine*, has been popular with college students, and is being used as supplemental reading at two universities. Married 40 years, he lives with Glenda in Woodbridge, CT.

Brandi Willis Schreiber

Brandi Willis Schreiber received her BA. in English Language and Literature and MA. in English (Creative Writing) from Texas Tech University. Her work has appeared in *The Texas Review, New Texas: A Journal of Culture and Literature, Red River Review, All Things Dickinson: An Encyclopedia of Emily Dickinson's World*, and elsewhere. Most recently, her short story, "The Family Tree," was published in *Second Chances: A Romance Writers of America Collection*. She currently works and writes from West Texas. You can connect with her at www.brandiwillisschreiber.com.

K.D. Van Brunt

K.D. Van Brunt has published five previous young adult books with small, independent publishers and is currently working on several exciting projects. His short story "Bang" was selected as first runner up for the 2015 SCBWI Magazine Merit Award, and his first book, *Win the Rings*, won the RWA's Fantasy, Futuristic and Paranormal award for the best book for 2015.

He's an active member of the RWA and SCBWI. His day job is lawyering, but his passion is telling a good tale and reading one. Learn more about K.D. Van Brunt here: http://www.kdvanbrunt.com.

Elizabeth G. Walzel

Elizabeth G. Walzel is the founder and CEO of *Writers Dialog*, and a cofounder of *2 Elizabeths*. She has been a member of the Board of Directors for Black Gold Surveying & Engineering, Inc. for 14 years. Beth admits to having an absolute addiction to reading and writing romance, and enjoys a great love for animals. She is most proud of her husband, Allen, and has been married for 32 happy years. She's also proud of her two amazing daughters, Elise and Meg. Learn more about Beth at www.WritersDialog.com.

Gerald Winter

Gerald Arthur Winter has a BA in Journalism from Rutgers University and an MFA in Creative Writing from the University of Tampa. His short stories have been published by *The Connotation Press, Hardboiled, The Creativity Webzine, 2 Elizabeths,* and *NY Literary Magazine* which published his story, "A Free Sampling," with a 5 Star Award for Meaningful Fiction in September 2016. To learn more about Gerald, visit his website here:
www.geraldarthurwinter.com.

Nancy Young

A former editor, reporter, and college educator, Nancy Young is the author of the *Something in the Dark* romantic suspense series: *Seeing Things, Hearing Things*, and *Sensing Things*. Her other works include a poetry chapbook, *The Last Girl Standing*, and dozens of poems, articles, and short stories that have appeared in various journals, magazines, newspapers, and anthologies. Nancy lives in Fuquay-Varina, where she raised four reasonably well-adjusted children and still lives with her husband Dan, her basset hound Opie, and her sullen cat.

Flash Fiction

Julia Ballerini
After leaving academe, Julia Ballerini turned to her long-derailed ambition: writing fiction. She's written several stories, three of which have been published. She's also revising a novel she thought was finished. She intends "In a Castle in France" as an undercover (literally) fable of feminist resistance.

Guy Biederman
Guy lives on a houseboat near San Francisco with his wife, daughter, and two salty cats where he practices tai chi and walks the planks daily. He began writing as a Peace Corps volunteer in Guatemala in 1981, was evacuated, and later received an MA. at San Francisco State, where his creative writing teaching career began. His work has appeared in many literary journals including *Carve, Third Wednesday, daCunha, Flash Frontier,* and *Sea Letter*. He prefers to write on matchbooks, ATM receipts with low balances, and parking tickets while waiting for traffic lights to change.

Six Word Stories 2E League Members

Heide Arbitter
Heide Arbitter's plays have been produced in New York City and regionally. She's published in *Smith & Kraus* and *Excalibur*. Short stories are published in *Adelaide Literary Magazine.*

Kirk Beeler
Kirk Beeler is a lifelong student and lover of short fiction. Lately, he has rekindled an energy for writing put aside for too many years of work. This is a new beginning.

Elizabeth Cockle
Elizabeth Cockle is a communications director at a digital marketing agency in Toronto. She side-hustles writing back-cover copy for romance novels, where everyone lives happily and sexily ever after. Elizabeth studied creative writing at The New School in New York City and is a cofounder of the *Dock Tales* spoken word series in Toronto's East End.

R.B. Frank
See her bio above.

Michel Krug
Michel Krug graduated from the Writing Seminars at the Johns Hopkins University. He writes poetry, literary fiction, was a print journalist and now practices law in St. Paul, MN. His poems have appeared in *The Lilith Review, Roachprint Anthology, Thirty West, November 2017, Main Street Rag, Brooklyn Review, Riverrun, Borealis, Poetry Motel* and *The Blind Man's Rainbow.*

Cindy Matthews

Cindy Matthews has worked as a chambermaid, potato peeler, data entry operator, teacher, and special education vice-principal. She writes, paints, and instructs online courses for teachers in her studio office in rural Ontario, Canada. Her writing has appeared online and in print in Canada, USA, UK, South Asia, South Africa, and Australia. You can learn more at http://www.cindymatthews.ca/about-cindy.

Phyllis McKinley

Phyllis McKinley is a word lover whose work has received multiple awards. She has four poetry books published and short nonfiction pieces in four *Florida Collections* and several *Chicken Soup for the Soul Books*. She is happy to be published now in Texas!

Mattie Lee Monroe

Mattie Lee Monroe is a nontraditional college student enrolled in a Creative Writing and History double major. She lives on the edge of the western North Dakota badlands and enjoys writing across genres. She won the Dickinson ND Area Library's 2015 Adult Short Story Contest. Her writing process involves a symbiotic relationship with Tabasco chocolate, Sudoku, and Mumford & Sons music.

Valerie J. Runyan

Valerie J. Runyan started writing in Los Angeles where she grew up. She raised her two adult children in Las Vegas where she also took up photography. She started her first blog and first podcast outside of Houston. She has returned to Las Vegas to continue her writing and publishing journey. Learn more about Valerie by visiting her website:

www.furiouswordsmith.blogspot.com.

Jeffrey H. Toney

Dr. Toney has published scientific peer-reviewed articles, news media opinion pieces as well as short fiction stories in *Sick Lit Magazine, O-Dark-Thirty,* the literary journal of *The Veterans Writing Project, The East Coast Literary Review, Crack The Spine, Storyland Literary Review, 600 Second Saga, No Extra Words* and in *2 Elizabeths*. Recently, he was nominated for a Pushcart Prize for his 100-word story, "The Quiet Raspberry Wormhole" in *Crack The Spine*, published in their recent anthology. He serves as Provost and Vice President for Academic Affairs at Kean University.

Gerald Winter

See his bio above.

Marlene Woods

Marlene Woods has been composing poetry since her adolescence. Her debut poetry collection about love and heartbreak titled *Not Love* will be published on February 28, 2018. She is a member of the 2E League at *2 Elizabeths* literary magazine. She writes poetry about her children at: www.themarlenecollection.com and poetry about romance and other personal experiences at www.iloveyougram.com. She currently resides in Virginia with her husband and three children. She loves writing, photography, scrapbooking, baking and is always on the hunt for cozy cafés serving delicious and good-looking cappuccinos.

Poetry

Margaritë Camaj
Margaritë Camaj never runs out of love. She grew up in the Bronx, New York, and has Albanian roots. Love, writing, and music have been her fuel through it all. Writing has been a part of Margaritë since she was seven years old and she has published seven books. Additionally, she is a NY Attorney who fights for human rights.

Hannah Fields
Fields is a writer and editor by profession and a coffee junkie by choice. When she isn't seeking out her next adventure, she is an avid reader, music enthusiast, and part-time poet.

Elise Holland
Elise Holland is a cofounder and the editor-in-chief of *2 Elizabeths*. Through *2 Elizabeths*, she's on a constant quest to create value and visibility for writers. Her work has appeared in several publications, some of which include *The Writer's Dig, DIY MFA,* and *Writer's Digest Magazine*. When she's not writing or editing, she can be found spending time with her sweet husband and very feisty chihuahua.

Michel Krug
See his bio above.

David Lukas
David Lukas lives in New York City where he works for Planned Parenthood Federation of America and trains competitively as a marathon runner.

Francesca Lupini

Francesca Lupini is originally from Rhode Island and is now studying psychology and creative writing at Saint Joseph's University in Philadelphia. She has been practicing writing since she was very young, but in the past few years began writing poetry more seriously as a result of a creative writing course she took at Marianapolis Preparatory School. She hopes to one day publish her own collection of poetry.

Lisa St. John

Lisa St. John is a high school English Teacher and published poet. Her newest endeavors include a memoir in progress and, of course, poetry. Her first chapbook, *Ponderings*, can be purchased at *Finishing Line Press*. She lives in the beautiful Hudson Valley of upstate New York where she calls the Catskill Mountains home. Lisa has published her poetry in the *Barbaric Yawp*, *Bear Creek Haiku*, *Misfit Magazine*, *The Poet's Billow PKA's Advocate*, *Haight Ashbury Literary Journal*, *The Ekphrastic Review*, and *Chronogram Magazine*. The poem "There Must Be a Science to This" won The Poet's Billow's Bermuda Triangle Contest and "Mowing the Lawn" was shortlisted for the Fish Poetry Prize and later published in *Fish Anthology 2016*. She also has several travel articles posted on GoNomad.com To learn more about Lisa visit her website, here: http://www.lisastjohnblog.com.